Thomas Edward Besolow

From the Darkness of Africa to the Light of America

The Story of an African Prince

Thomas Edward Besolow

From the Darkness of Africa to the Light of America
The Story of an African Prince

ISBN/EAN: 9783744799317

Printed in Europe, USA, Canada, Australia, Japan

Cover: Foto ©Andreas Hilbeck / pixelio.de

More available books at **www.hansebooks.com**

Darkness of Africa

to the

Light of America

The Story of an African Prince

BY

THOMAS E. BESOLOW

"Breathes there a man with soul so dead,
Who never to himself hath said,
'This is my own, my native land'?"

BOSTON

FRANK WOOD, PRINTER, 352 WASHINGTON STREET

1891

INTRODUCTION.

In the spring term of 1887, when it was my good fortune to be enrolled as a student in "Old Wesleyan," at Wilbraham, it was my privilege to meet for the first time, Mr. Besolow. Never before had I grasped the hand, or looked into the face, of a native of Africa. Since that time I have been thankful that the Divine Providence brought me into the presence of one who had lived in the darkness of Africa, as long as I had lived in the light of America.

My acquaintance with Mr. Besolow, which for more than three years has been very intimate, has been very pleasant and profitable.

Mr. Besolow, as a student, has indeed done honor to his race, If the moral and mental caliber of this son of Africa is a fair sample of his race, then the Negro is a man, in many respects, not inferior to the Anglo-Saxon. We, who know him, believe that in the future the world will hear from him, and that good "Old Wesleyan Academy" will yet be proud of having nourished within her walls this negro brother.

Considering that most of us have always lived amid the rush of our own hasty American life, and under the influence of our mighty, Christian civilization, have we not, in some measure, failed to behold the great and many needs of the millions who in Africa are enjoying the smallest volume of life, because the superstition and the heathenism of darker ages rule them with an iron sceptre, which bends them to the dust, and urges them to worship and to implore a cold, dead, barren moon to bless them, and to guide them?

Away down through this brazen superstition, through the empty idolatry, and into the heart and mind of this humble African, there beamed a golden ray of the marvelous, life-giving light of the Saviour of the world. His whole soul became illuminated with the light of truth. Many have heard his humble testimony of how God redeemed him from the idolatry and human sacrifices of his people.

Mr. Besolow is indeed a living, marvelous example of God's miraculous power to enlighten the heart and mind of man; to enable him to see the utter absurdity in bowing down to wood and stone, and on the other hand to enable him to know the far-reaching felicity of worshiping Jehovah's Son.

Mr. Besolow is a prince. By legal right, it is his to occupy the throne which was once his father's. Behold, readers of this little book, what might then be accomplished toward the uplifting, the edifying, and the saving of these millions of souls for whom Christ died. In a few years Mr. Besolow will go out from beneath the domes of the institutions of learning in America, and he will possess an education such as few, if any, of his countrymen have hitherto acquired. Where will he go? It is his hope to drink, for a time, from the " Pierean stream " as it flows from the halls of learning in Europe. Where then will he go?

All hearts who may then know him will say, " God bless him," as he returns, a Christian prince, to the land that gave him birth. It is his hope to regain the power which belongs to him, and having regained it, to swing open wide the gates, through which the Christian missionary from every land may pass, and tell the wondrous story of the Son of God to all his race. It behooves us to remember that.Africa is still dark. And the darkness which is yet brooding over that benighted people is of such density, as never can be conceived by one who was born, and has always lived, in a Christian nation like our own.

Think of the long line of deluded women, who have given themselves as sacrifices, to be buried beside the body of a king or chieftain, deeming it a high honor to be thus entombed alive by the side of a dead ruler. Consider the thousands of human beings who have been sacrificed to the moon, as their fellow-citizens made their vows to that " pale Empress of the night." And remember, that, as you peruse the lines of this little book, the millions of that vast African world are struggling beneath the awful thraldom of this empty religion.

Christianity has taught Mr. Besolow the great heaven-born principle of the universal brotherhood of man. In his heart burns the quenchless fire of true patriotism, which nerves him to struggle against mighty odds, to uplift, enlighten and Christianize his countrymen.

He is aiding with funds, which he has accumulated by hard labor and self-sacrifice, and the kindness of influential men and women, several young men and young women, both white and black, to qualify themselves to go with him to Africa, and work among his people. He intends, if Providence gives him life and success, and if Christian men will sustain him, to be instrumental in building schools and colleges, especially in Soudan and Guinea, to give his countrymen a Christian education.

In the lecture field, for a young man, he has had a rich and helpful experience, which is ever broadening before him. He has lectured before the students of Wellesley and Harvard colleges, and at this present writing he has an engagement to lecture on Africa before the Divinity School at Yale College.

In all of the great work which he has planned regarding Africa, there can be no selfish motive, for it is by long days of incessant toil that he is laboring, amid all of his other duties, to complete his own education, while at the same time he is helping relatives and friends, with the hope that they will go with him and assist in carrying out his plans to help his very needy people. In all of his endeavors, the one grand purpose which fills his active mind, and upon which his eyes are irrevocably fixed, as upon a brilliant star in the midst of a blackened sky, is the enlightenment and the Christianization of his race.

Noble ambition! Grander than Napoleon's! As worthy as Paul's! Upon a throne in the heart of Africa, with Christ reigning upon the throne of his heart, with the flame of Christian civilization burning in his mind, will not Mr. Besolow make that darkened world feel his existence for its advancement?

I firmly believe that no one who has moved, or may move, to aid him in his noble plans in behalf of his countrymen, will ever know a moment to regret having thus moved.

Go on thy mission, little book, and may the instruction on thy pages borne, find lodgment in the heart of every reader. And may the touching scenes of empty idol worship, and human sacrifices, there recorded, turn hearts and eyes toward Africa, and inspire all to help, as best we can, that needy race.

WARREN F. LOW,
A classmate, friend, and brother to Mr. Besolow.

WESLEYAN ACADEMY, WILBRAHAM, MASS.,
Nov. 12, 1890.

PREFACE.

It was in a mission school, Cape Mount, Africa, that for the first time the truth dawned upon me that there was a higher civilization, and that the God whom I had worshiped from my childhood was not the true God. This star of my vision I have followed until I find myself in this great and highly favored land. Here I am struggling to secure an education for myself, cousin, and a few young men of my native Africa, that we may go back to our people and assure them that the glory of the Lord has risen indeed upon the Western Nation,—such as we hope may be true some day of our own land.

In this place I wish to mention my appreciation to the Congregational, Methodist, Presbyterian, and Baptist Churches of the United States, and to thank the young men of Harvard, Yale, and Williams Colleges, and the young ladies of Wellesley College.

My sincere thanks are especially extended to the Shawmut Congregational Church, Boston, Mass., New Old South, Back Bay, Boston, Phillips Congregational Church, South Boston, Immanuel Congregational Church, Roxbury, M. E. Church, Lenox, Mass., Park Street Church, Springfield, Mass., Fourth Congregational Church, Hartford, Conn., South Congregational Church, Concord, N. H., M. E. Church, Gloversville, N. Y., and the Hyde Park Congregational Church, Jermain Memorial Church, West Troy, N. Y.

I take this opportunity, also, to thank Miss M. Annie Wythe, Preceptress of Wesleyan Academy, and all others who assisted me in my work, which thing I failed to do in my former edition. Also, the friends who have kindly criticised my pamphlet, and called my attention to the errors. The foregoing all have my deepest gratitude for the kindness they have shown me, and for the help afforded me.

Through lack of finances I was compelled to cut down the manuscript which I had prepared, from three hundred to one hundred and twenty-six pages. Being ill, and absent from my regular abode, I intrusted this work to a person whom I thought was competent, as she had done considerable copying for me. She afterward read the proof, as I was busy with studies and my lecture; but as she did not understand the ins and outs of my country, gross errors naturally found their way into my pamphlet. It is my purpose in this edition to correct these mistakes, and present to the American people, as true as it is possible for me to tell it, a vivid representation of the manners and customs of my people, and the story of my own life.

Some descriptions written herein may appear on the face as impossible, or at least exaggerated, but I assure you my dear reader they are facts. If I should tell you other scenes which I have witnessed you would wonder the more; suffice it to say that Henry M. Stanley's work will bear me out in some of my assertions.

If this brief account of my people and the story of my own life shall awaken in any an interest in my people, I shall be profoundly thankful, and one end of my writing will be accomplished. Whatever returns will be realized from the sale of this little book, will be spent in securing an education for the work awaiting me in the "Dark Continent," which is beckoning me on with an impatient cry. The remainder, if any, in swelling the fund for the building of an institution for my people which will be a centre of light to dispel the darkness of ignorance from their minds, and which will be a monument for what "the God of the righteous" has done for a son of Africa.

This book, therefore, is sent forth with prayer that God may use the thoughts within it to his own glory, for multiplying the so-much-needed laborers in that part of his vineyard, and that the day may soon dawn when those heinous sacrifices will be obliterated forever from the continent of my dearest Africa, and that the land of my birth may no longer be termed the "Dark Continent," but the "Beacon Light" of the whole world.

In my former edition, it will be remembered by those who read it, I mentioned my intention to bring my only brother, a lad of fourteen years, to this country. To my disappointment, I received a letter from him which will be found in the last chapter of this pamphlet, stating that he would not come. I hope, however, that by continued inducements I may be able to change his mind. My prayer is that God will send him here. Let all my Christian friends pray to this end. If the kind people who sent me money for his passage will write to me, and so desire it, I shall remit their money; if not, it will be added to the building money, providing my brother decides not to come.

In regard to my school, I thank God I am winning an interest for it from the influential men of my part of Africa. Some of their names may be found in the chapter devoted to the institution.

I am grateful for this fact, that this pamphlet has found its way into the White House, to the Astors, and to the New England peasants. It has crossed the deep to Her Majesty the Queen of England, to Hon. William E. Gladstone, and other Lords of the British Empire. Further, it has entered other parts of Europe: it is in the hands of Emperor William and Prince Bismarck of Germany, kings of Denmark, Scandinavia, and Austria, and our special friend, who has opened Congo Free State, Leopold II., of Belgium, who loves dear Africa's soil. It has gone to other principal potentates of Europe, even to the Czar of Russia and the Khedive of Egypt.

Truly, then, I can say,—

> "While eternal ages watch and wait,
> God's plans move on."

Yours for Christ and Africa,

THOMAS E. BESOLOW,

Wilbraham, Mass.

Address all orders for pamphlets, etc., to Thomas E. Besolow, 61 South Street, Boston, Mass.

Please inclose five cents in stamps for postage.

CHAPTER I.

Esne amicus Dei bona fide, opere in terra incognita et populo Æthiopiæ?

PHYSICAL AND ETHNOLOGICAL AFRICA.

In giving a general description of Africa, we must depend largely upon the accounts of men who have traveled over the country more or less. No one man has been able or ever will be able to travel over the whole continent, visiting its every part. The account of one traveler, be it ever so broad and comprehensive, conveys, after all, but a slight idea of the magnitude of this grand division of the land. To obtain an at all comprehensive idea of Equatorial, Western Central, Northern and Southern Africa, we must read with careful thought and study the writings of such authorities as Mungo Parke, Speke, Burton, Moffat, Livingstone, Stanley, and hosts of other and lesser lights whose works are authentic enough to be worthy the careful reading of a student on Africa and the African problem.

Now while this pamphlet pertains wholly to myself and my own tribe, I feel that I should like to repeat a few of the general statements that have been made upon Africa, especially upon Physical Africa,—and I would also like to occupy a brief space on the people of that continent. A few brief ideas, or as the Roman has it, "multum in parvo." The continent under consideration, as all students of geography know, is one of the five grand divisions of the globe and ranks second in size. An English writer says, "larger than North and South America." It is the largest peninsula in the world. It is about 6,000 miles long, and 5,000 miles in width at its widest part, and it contains about 11,000,000 square miles of surface. It has about 17,000 miles of coast land; but the coast is very regular, being broken but by few gulfs and bays; perhaps this is one of the reasons why the interior is so little known to the white men. Its Temperate Zone occupies a space of about 1,000 miles. Its extreme southern part lies in the South Temperate Zone. It has a central belt of 40,000 square miles which lies in the Torrid Zone.

The greater part of Africa is, of course, in the Torrid Zone ; and, as much of the country is desert-land, it is, in general, the hottest and driest of all the continents. Africa may easily be divided into five divisions. Northern and Eastern, Southern and Western and Central Africa. Northern Africa includes the Barbary States, the countries of the Nile, and Sahara the great Sandy Desert. The principal food plant in the region of Barbary States is the date-palm. Indeed, this kind of tree is so prolific that the southern part of the States is called " Beled-el-jerid," meaning "Land of Dates." Other products of the States are grain, cotton, and Morocco leather. From the interior caravans bring ivory, ostrich feathers and gold-dust.

You have all heard, I have no doubt, of that remarkable portion of the surface, known as the Desert of Sahara. This vast table-land is about three fifths the size of the United States. Though the greater part of the desert is a sandy, scorchingly hot plain, it does have places of much beauty here and there on its bosom. Oases are scattered over its surface at irregular distances. From some of these oases rise low and swelling hills and even mountain groups. Here also are found large and luxuriant groves of trees of the date and palm family, and amidst these, sheltered by green, cool vines, are fresh and bubbling springs, the Mecca of the desert traveler.

Prosperous little towns and villages are found on some of these oases, and on others good grain and fruit are raised. It seems hard to realize, and yet it is truth, that on some of these fertile spots in the very centre of the desert are cultivated groves of peaches, pomegranates, oranges, apples, bananas, barley, clover and tobacco. That such articles of commerce as peaches, barley and apples should grow in such a clime seems incredible, and yet you will find that Henry M. Stanley, Mungo Parke, and many German travelers, as well as missionaries to Africa will testify to the truth of my words. Artesian wells are easily obtained, and many hundreds of them are to be found by the weary, thirsty traveler, gushing fountain-like from the ground.

The Nile Countries are Egypt, Nubia, Kordofan and Abyssinia, the most important of these being Egypt. Yes, Egypt celebrated above all lands ! Africa feels justly proud of you. Proud of your noble pyramids—your stately ruins of old and ancient and decayed temples and cities. Egypt occupies the northeastern part of Africa, and extends from the Mediterranean to the source of the Nile, and lies between the Red Sea and Sahara. "The Delta " is a fertile spot found in the Nile about forty miles inward, and this is a most remarkably rich, productive and pleasant spot, and is comparatively speaking under good cultivation. Rain is never known in the valley of the Nile ; but for two, or more, often three months of every year the waters of the great river rise slowly until they overflow its banks and make the valley from the mountains to the sea look more like a huge lake than anything else. When this water settles away from the land again, the people plant their fields. These soon become green and beautiful, and yield abundantly. Among the principal products of this region are cotton, rice and wheat.

Central Africa is about three thousand miles in width. It is heavily timbered. Here are found the densest of jungles, and some of the trees measure through from surface to surface anywhere from one to six feet. Vines of various families entwine about the trees from top to bottom. They knit the trees so closely together, that it is only an experienced African traveler or a native African, who can make any kind of headway through them. No one but one who has seen it, can imagine and realize what the real density of such a forest is like. When the sun is at its zenith, these forests, which never feel its warmth nor are brightened by its light, are filled with a dampness like that of death, and a gloom like that of night ; the leaves of the trees are always covered with night-time dews. While passing through such a forest, much suffering is endured from the intense cold. Oftentimes, as I have taken a short journey through them, my hands have turned nearly white with the cold ; so benumbed have they become that I could scarcely move them, and with all my exertions, I could not get any life into them till I climbed upon high ground, where a few, faint rays of the sun would reach my chilled body and thaw it out somewhat. In this manner Stanley and his men suffered much, as I have no doubt my reader is very well aware.

The whole country is not covered with so thick a forest as the one described, but there are many of them, and where they are found the population is sparse and most degraded. If God's sunshine could get to the land ; if it could penetrate the thick leaves of the trees, and dry the foul moisture thereon, it would be a different country. If it could be cleared, the progress would be remarkable. The portion which has been cleared has been cultivated with much success.

The physical resources of Africa are adequate to sustain a large population. Indeed, the resources for sustenance and wealth are truly wonderful. The soil is rich and extremely productive. Crops can be grown at all times throughout the year, and from one year to another unceasingly. The soil seems to hold its richness in a remarkble manner that many cannot understand.

The people of Africa are various and heterogeneous. There is a great mixture of tribes and nationalities, especially in the more northern parts, and more especially in the Barbary States. However, the Moors predominate ; while there are many Jews and Turks. The prevailing religion as you might infer from the foregoing is the Mohammedan form ; but the Jewish and Roman Catholic creeds are also very strong. Protestant religion and missions are fighting against great odds, but they are doing good work and making headway in these States. I feel that I ought right here to mention some few things concerning the mission work. Information on this subject is needed coming from whatever source it may. Needed to awaken a greater interest and enthusiasm in the " Dark Continent " and also to awaken to more active work ; and also to give information to inquiring minds,—minds that are interested in the awakening country. If my attempt at doing so is humble, it still is something, and shows, at least, that one heart is loyal to the continent of possibilities—that one heart is beating with love for a benighted people, that one head and two hands are willing to labor night and day, and do their part in uprooting superstition and error from the African land, and from the hearts of the African people, whether it be the superstition of creeds or of heathenism. Yes, I firmly believe, and my belief is fixed by observation, that the Protestants are doing all in their power to spread the Gospel of the Lord among these benighted people ; but it is hard and difficult work. In the way of building churches and schools, they are doing good work—truly wonderful work— when you pause to consider all the difficulties they have to overcome, and all the impediments and obstacles thrown in their path by those whose sympathies are not with them.

These impediments are bravely cast aside, and the obstacles

surmounted with patient persistency. Anything is possible to a man or woman who has the love of God in his or her heart, and who has a strong will for the right—

> "The strength to dare — the nerve to meet
> Whatever threatens with defeat—
> Is all indomitable will."

Success to these brave, Protestant people! May the choicest rewards crown their noble efforts is the earnest prayer of one whom they have helped to civilization. It is not an easy thing to work among these mixed tribes. Some tribes in Northern Africa, not properly speaking the Soudan, are treacherous, war-like and full of barbarity.

Amalgamative people of Northern Africa are more desirous of plunder than some other tribes in Guinea, such as the Mandingoes and the Veys, and as these are my own people, I feel that I would like to speak in a general way concerning them. In the first place the Mandingoes and Vey tribes are one and the same. They inhabit a district which extends from 8° to 12° north latitude, and is situated between the head-waters of the Senegal and Niger Rivers, comprising a population of anywhere from 6,000,000 to 8,000,000 souls. As a people there is nothing lazy or shiftless about them. They have, if I may be allowed to say it, capabilities for a high degree of civilization and have very good ideas of organization.

They have fixed dwellings, and though they are in most cases merely mud huts, they are usually defended by stockades. They are possessed of some laws and customs which are most favorable to commerce. The land is cultivated to some extent, and gold and iron are manufactured into various articles with much nicety of execution and much ingenuity. Cloth is also woven and dyed. Altogether they have qualities which speak well for the uplifting of the standard of life in Africa. They are the most widely circulated and important peoples of West Africa, north of the Equator, and are, I think, the best representatives you would find of the Negro stock.

A great many people are under the impression that the native man of Central Africa, irrespective of the tribe to which he belongs, neither toils nor spins nor cultivates the land, nor provides and procures for himself those things which are requisite for sustaining his body. These impressions are erroneous as you will find, if you proceed with this little book.

It is mostly the native man who has hewn down the dark forests of which I have made mention, and thus permitted the light of heaven to warm the cold soil into life and vigor. A great many men have been misled about the negro or true black man. I do not mean to exhibit any prejudice, because I do not believe that a man can be a true Christian and yet be a prejudiced one at the same time. " He that holds malice with his neighbor not only causes his neighbor to be at variance with him but he destroys his own soul." Generally, one will find in this land of America, the poorest representatives of African people, proper. They have been for centuries degraded by slavery and kept down by prejudice till they have become, some of them at least, but little higher than the lower animals. Whose fault is this? Ask yourself this question, my dear reader. Is it the American negro's fault, or is it rather his misfortune? Have there not come, even out of such poor material, men whom the world has marked as men of rare intellect, and fair representatives of what the entire race will finally become?

Poor morals, groveling obedience to any command, benumbed intellect and shiftless habits are not the characteristics of an African who has been given opportunities for self-advancement. These failings and faults which you see in the American negro have been caused by cruelty and bondage, and the hard usage received while they were for so many years the slaves of white masters, and white masters are responsible. Our brothers will pay the penalty, just as Rome did. Their intellectual powers have been crushed by it—their morals crippled by it—their habits and customs and modes of living lowered and degraded by it; in short, all that was highest, noblest, and worthiest of cultivation has been crushed out of their hearts and souls until nothing is left that was their own by prerogative, save their sunny, happy dispositions. You say the negro man is lazy. Granted. What is the cause of this fact? Until thirty years ago, more or less, what incentive did he have to become anything higher than the beast of burden, which, in the eyes of his white master, he was. Of what use was it for him to show himself ambitious, progressive and active? If he did so he would be termed a " smart nigger," and his reward would be the auction block, where because of these very qualities, he would bring a bigger price to his master.

You say that he has no intellect. What was done to enlarge

and cultivate his mental powers until the Civil War? Where for him and his were the schools and the advantages for learning such as the white children had? For the negro, the slave, in the very happiest and most prosperous moments what was there beyond a hoe, cotton-picking, three scanty meals a day, his bare hut at night, and his banjo? Do you think, kind reader, that you ought to judge of the possibilities of the African people by their unfortunate representatives found in this country? Why, there are some tribes in the interior of Africa that have never come into contact with Christianity or civilization and its influences; but they are not idle or shiftless. They cultivate their own lands, invent their own alphabets, make their own hoes, and are superior to American negroes in intellect. Also plant corn, make their own fibre; tan leather, and make it into sandals for their feet.

Others in the Western sections, including my own tribe, obtain ore. When iron they melt it and work it over into sabres and spears and various other articles. From gold ore, they make finger rings and amulets. Most certainly these are signs that there is something in the African man capable of cultivation, and demanding the respect and attention of the civilized world. The day is not far distant when the sable man will shine forth with that intelligence, knowledge, education and the love of God, such as will give him a place among the enlightened men of the world. I *know* that, with God's gracious sanction, my prophecy will come to pass. This is a self-evident fact—that the negro in his original state is a man of some intellect; but when forced into slavery and bondage, he becomes demoralized in every respect, for which he is not responsible, for he cannot help himself. The white man is blameworthy.

The attention of civilization has been directed toward the continent for nearly one hundred years, now; but nothing has been accomplished that amounted to much of anything, until within the last sixty years. Within that time Africa has been somewhat evangelized, Christianized. Good people have during this time established colonies on her borders; namely, Liberia and Congo, which have been the home of liberated slaves for more than eighty years. These colonies have been partly supported, and ministers have been sent there, by these benefactors. Teachers, consecrated men and women, have gone out for the purpose of redeeming the land. Now, at this present time, the colonies are able to sustain themselves and their various institutions of learning and their creed ; and are sending light and salvation to those who sit in darkness.

In the colonies there have been established common schools, grammar schools and seminaries and academies, in which the young may be trained for the purpose of teaching. Robert Moffat, who, I suppose, was the first missionary to those dark parts of the land, carried to the natives, as early as 1816, the blessed gospel light. Heroes have struggled, labored and died since then for the continent, trying to establish within its borders the religion of Jesus Christ. Do not despair, and say in discouraged tones, the African man will never amount to anything. Have patience ; teach him of the love of Christ and teach him to love humanity ; labor patiently—labor, labor and "learn to labor and to wait." Labor and patience go hand in hand.

Take all superscriptions on Egyptian images and paintings, and you will find that all persons represented thereon resemble your humble servant. We have the same physiognomy. Two years ago, while I was standing in New York Central Park, my attention was called to an Egyptian obelisk ; and as I looked at the superscription, and hieroglyphics on the pillar, I could trace a strong similarity to those used among the Veys and Mandingoes ; whether they are exactly equivalent in meaning, I cannot presume to say.

VEY HIEROGLYPHICS.

It may be interesting to notice the similarity of the Vey language with other languages. Take, for instance, the English word "lamp" and the corresponding Greek word "lampas," in the Vey it is "lampo." Take the English word "call" and the corresponding Greek word "kaleo," and Latin "calare." Danish "Kalleu," the Vey is "kally." Notice the cognate mutes. Other examples are the English word "phase ;" in Greek it is "phaino," and in the Vey "phala." Also, Sanskrit "asmi," Greek "emmi," Latin "sum," the Vey "amme." The English "dear" is "dearmo" in Vey. The English word "litany," with the corresponding words in French are " littanie," Spanish "litania," Greek "litaenein," and the Vey is "litca." The Greek word "ite," meaning "to go," in Vey is "ite." The corresponding words for the English "father," in German is "vater," in Vey is "fath." The Vey for the English "mother" is "moth," while in Greek it is "mater," and in Latin "mater."

Would that I had the money, I would educate twenty-five or thirty colored young men, and take them home with me for work there. I am laboring now very hard to see a young man and brother, Stewart by name, through an education. He is a native of this country, and of Springfield, Mass. He is in Wilbraham with me. He is a young man of remarkable ability, but has never had any opportunity for going to school until now. My soul burns to help and encourage him. He and I work together, and if I can persuade him to go to Africa to work in the large field there I shall do so.

> "Ye whose hearts are fresh and simple,
> Who have faith in God and Nature,
> Who believe that in all ages
> Every human heart is human,
> That in even savage bosoms
> There are longings, yearnings, strivings
> For the good they comprehend not,
> That the feeble hands and helpless,
> Groping blindly in the darkness,
> Touch God's right hand in that darkness
> And are lifted up and strengthened
> Listen to this simple story."
>
> —*Song of Hiawatha.*

CHAPTER II.

CHILDHOOD.

"There was a place in childhood,
    That I remember well;
And there a voice of sweetest tone,
    Bright wondrous tales did tell."
                                   —*Sam. Lover.*

CHILDHOOD AND SOME LEGENDS OF MY PEOPLE.

I was born in Bendoo, Upper Guinea, Africa. Just when, I do not know. From the best of my knowledge it was in 1867. No town clerk entered the fact upon his record—no wise census-taker put me down in his great book. Bendoo babies are born and then just grow. That's me. No trouble about clothes—no christening—no Sunday-school; day comes and day goes—all were just the same. I never was taught a, b, c. Imagine and picture to yourself a naked little urchin rolling around under foot, mouth full of sand, at times, and feet in air, and playing as children play the world over be they heathen or Christian; happy and miserable by turns, making little trouble, needing little care. I looked more like a big black spider than anything else, and grew to be a strong child.

The old women of my town were very fond of telling me stories of my extremely young youth; and I very much enjoyed listening to them, and questioned them minutely on points about which their memory seemed rather rusty. They told me at the tender age of two I came to blows with another infant pugilist. I was very hardy and lusty, and in this my first contest came off victorious. This may or may not be true; I hope it is not; but that Vey boys and girls begin to exercise their muscles in wrestling feats that are not always of a friendly nature, I cannot deny. Before I grew to the realization that I possessed pugilistic powers, I spent the time in a leather cradle, or pouch-like bag, that was fastened on my mother's back by tough leathern thongs.

This cradle was handsomely embroidered with red, white, and blue beads, and warmly lined with the softest cotton. I very much doubt if a civilized baby has better accommodations for the first months of his life than I had, according to the telling of those old women of whom I have told you. You see, my mother was of very high birth, and was the first wife of a king. In my country such a woman does not have the hard duties to perform which fall to the lot of the women of lower rank. I see the same distinction is made also in this country. Now, a woman of the lower class would have been obliged to go into the fields, with her child strapped upon her back, and to dig, and labor at burning brush or clearing woods all day long. The infant's face in the meantime would be pretty well blistered by the sun's scorching rays.

Such hardships were not the lot of my mother; she stayed in the shade and took good care of me, so that my early hours were the luxurious ones of a young prince. As I recall my mother, she was a tall, large, finely-proportioned woman, who showed in her every movement traces of her royal birth. She was the daughter of a neighboring king; indeed, she was a descendant of the same line of kings as my father; *i. e.*, the Goolah and Vey tribes. According to the custom of her tribe — and the same custom is in vogue in Vey — she was taught to sew, to embroider, and to cook; also how to fish in small lakes and ponds. All these things mother learned when very young. Because she was the daughter of a king, she was taught in addition to these things, to write the ideographs of our language; *i. e.*, each letter is equivalent to a word. She was taught at home in this way for four or five years; then she was isolated from the town and no one saw her again for several years. There she was taught household duties, as are all girls who attend the school. That much we all of us know; but what other things they are taught, or what they do during these long years, mother would never divulge. Any Vey woman would gladly die before she would whisper, even to her husband, the secrets of that period of her life. No man knows concerning it; for men are not allowed to go within an eighth of a mile of the retreat, on pain of death. After mother had spent these years in isolation, she came back with others to the capital town of the Goolah territory, and was ready to be purchased as a wife.

Being of royal birth, the price set for her was so high that no one but a prince or king could hope to possess her.

Father saw her when she was first home, and fell in love with her. Two years afterwards he went to his parents, as all Vey men are obliged to do when they wish to marry a woman, and told them he wanted her for his wife. They never make any advances towards a girl till they have first seen their own parents. Then father's parents went to negotiate with mother's, and asked them if Jessa could be purchased for their son. Mother's parents consented, and father married mother, and established her at Bendoo, where by right of her birth she held the first place among the rest of his wives.

The matter of purchasing a wife may be of interest to my readers. If the girl has learned a trade, i. e., if she has been taught to cook, to sew, to embroider, or to dress hair (and many women do nothing else but go about plaiting hair), if she is a dancer or singer, then her prospective husband is charged for her education. If she has been ill, they charge him for the medicine man's fee, also for the trouble they have had taking care of her during her illness.

If the man happens to be one of wealth, even her board from the day of her birth to the time of his marriage is put down in the bill. Then these are summed up, and if the young man has good habits — that is, if he does not steal nor lie, and can pay the bill — he takes possession of the girl. In our territory, as you might infer, there occur but few divorces. If he is able to pay the bill five times over, however, and is known to be a thief or a liar, he is not given the girl; for the things that a Vey man hates most are thieving and lying. For these crimes men are put to death.

My mother, Jessa, was distinguished in a great many ways from the other women of my tribe. She had never seen civilized people nor civilized countries, but as I look back and think over some things that were characteristic of her, I can readily see that she had ideas of a civilization rather of an advancement much higher than our own. She was a strict disciple of that old maxim "Cleanliness is next to godliness," and looked after our bodies with as scrupulous neatness as any lady mother could. This kind of care for their children was an exception, not a rule, among most of the mothers of Bendoo. In times of illness, or when hurt or wounded in some way, she would take care of us with the most tender solicitude,—sometimes would watch beside her sick child all night long, and all the following day. I remember once I had a kind of swamp fever and was very sick. She remained by me constantly, moistening my lips with cooling water, raising my burning head at times to a resting-place upon her bosom, and smoothing my aching brow with her soft, gentle hand.

Most Vey mothers would have called the medicine-man of the tribe to mutter his incantations and cast his spells over the sick child, and would not have troubled themselves further over its needs; but not so with my dear mother, my dear Jessa. After a Vey baby became old enough to run around and look after himself to a certain extent, some mothers almost literally washed their hands of him, left him to his own devices, and went about their business, seeming to have lost much of the motherly love and instinct that should have been natural to them. Like a dog that tires of its puppy, or a cat that wearies of its kitten, so a savage, uncivilized mother used oftentimes to grow tired of her offspring.

Here again was my mother a striking contrast to the women about her. She loved us all most tenderly: yes, I may say tenderly; it is not too strong nor too meaningful a word, for she did love us with all the yearning affection of which a mother is capable, and we loved her much in return. After all, though, as I have said above, there are exceptions; the Vey mother is characterized by her care of her young; and comparatively speaking is more advanced in this respect than many of the women of other African tribes. I think the capacity for devoted love, and for its reception in the heart, is a peculiarity of the Vey people; and the power of this emotion has a fine humanizing effect upon my people, and causes me to hope great things for them. I do not think that it will be a very difficult matter to implant in their bosoms a strong worship of Christ, and I mean to try it. But I diverge from the subject at hand. To go back to it once more. I remember how much I missed my mother when she died, and how bitterly I and my brothers and sisters mourned over her death. Yes, even now on my inward eye forming the "bliss of solitude," come her kind eyes and smile.

Father had over a hundred wives, but among them all his favorite was a woman called Taradobah. Father loved this woman more than he loved my mother and all of his other wives put together, and she seemed to return his affection. She was of high birth and of good ancestry like my mother, and she was a very handsome woman. Tall and straight, with muscles as hard and finely developed as a man. A well-shaped head set firmly upon a pair of grandly sloping shoulders. Her features were clearly and distinctly cut; her mouth had the firmness of a man's, and no one could stand before the direct, searching gaze of her quick, black eye. I saw a picture of the Medea of Grecian mythology, and though she was white, there was something about her commanding air that called up Taradobah to my mind.

Taradobah was indeed born to command. She was not an average woman, and was not to fill an average place in the world. Perhaps because of her love for my father, she loved all his children. At any rate, she formed a strong attachment for me, and I for her, and I was fond of playing around outside of her hut with her children and my half-brothers and half-sisters. When I was older, she told me, if ever I needed a friend, I should find it in her; and I remembered those words afterwards.

The lessons mother taught my brothers and myself about the respect we owed father, and submission to his will in all things, live always in my memory. From an infant, or from the time I could think, I was taught to do cheerfully and willingly all that my father bade me do, whether it was right or wrong. Indeed, my ideas of the distinction between right and wrong were imperfectly developed, if at all.

Disobedience in the young was considered the most flagrant of offenses, and it was not only my father who could punish me for disobedience, but any man of forty or fifty years of age could thrash me soundly; and when I recall the blows that so often fell upon my back, you will understand that my being a prince made no difference in regard to chastisement. No clemency was shown to me because of my rank. I suffered in common with the other boys and girls of more lowly parentage.

A willing, cheerful obedience to our elders was required, or else we suffered harsh, and often horrible punishments, such as make me shudder now as I think of them.

How many times have I beheld with tear-filled eyes and sympathetic heart, some young companion tied hand and foot to a post for some childish misdemeanor.. He was left there for hours with the hot rays of the burning sun pouring down upon his uncovered head and body,— sun, too, so hot as to shrivel into nothingness the very leaves upon the trees, at times.

Here he would hang, sometimes, if he was thought worthy of severer treatment than usual, till he was almost exhausted for want of food and drink. I have known some boys to remain tied in such manner for a day at a time; and remember, a day is twelve hours with us.

We would stand at a distance, and look at him with the utmost pity in our eyes, and with sorrowing hearts; but we dared not approach too near to him, or offer him any food; for if we did, we would suffer like punishment, with an extra blow or two thrown in.

Sometimes an iron is heated to a white heat, and the miserable little culprit is made to take the iron thus heated in his hand. It burns deeply into the flesh, and if he does not lose his whole hand, he loses the use of it for a long, long time, and carries the scar for life. I am happy to say that the palms of my hands are not scarred in this way, but there are scars on my arms.

Ah, I can now, in my imagination, hear again the wails and moans of those unfortunate children, and can experience now as I did then the sickening sensation of fear and disgust at sound of their cries. A parent can have a child slain for disobedience or disrespect. I remember one little fellow — he was just my own age, and we roamed the woods and played our games together, and had a strong affection one for the other. The first bitter grief of my life was when Tano's head was almost taken off by an angry father for a real or fancied impertinence.

You can see what unlimited power a parent has over his children, and how severe is the discipline of a Vey African boy. Yes, and girl, too, for the sex makes no difference. It is not much to be wondered at that they become such fearless, brave soldiers and huntsmen, when you consider the severity in which they have been trained, and how from earliest childhood they are constantly seeing cruel and bloody affairs like the kind mentioned above.

You may understand, then, that we boys and girls were very careful not to give offense and to obey always. The Vey boys stand in much fear and trepidation of their elders, and

have the utmost respect for them.   I often think that the African boy might give the civilized boy and girl a few lessons in
showing respect and reverence to those who are older than
themselves, and especially the Yankee boy.

I was very swift-footed, and had the extreme honor, for so
it was considered, of being the one among all the boys of my
own age who could run the most rapidly and run the longest
distance without becoming tired.

Though we were all bare-footed, the soles of our feet
became so tough and hard from constant usage that they were
very soon insensible to pain, and I cannot remember that I
complained of any hurt—the tough skin being impenetrable
even to sharp thorns.

When I was eight years of age I was taught how to use the
bow and arrows.   The proudest day of my life was when I
became the owner for the first time of a bow and a quiver of
nicely sharpened arrows.   What gay times we used to have, in
spite of all the constant, ever lurking fear of punishment, which
we could not shake off.   Remember, a boy that is nine years
old is pretty large in my country.

Sometimes fifty, often one hundred of us boys, would
practice shooting at a target, standing at a distance of forty
feet or more.   The target was a round piece of tiger skin,
with a diameter of about one inch and a half.   The boys would
shoot at this target in turn, the boy whose arrow pierced the
bull's-eye taking all the arrows of those who had tried before
him and failed.   Often when I was the lucky boy, the others
would cheer me till they were hoarse, carry me on their shoulders about the town, and placing a wreath of palm leaves about
my forehead, after the manner of the early Greeks in their
sports, would declare me a hero or a king.   I cannot tell you
with what a glow of pride and dignity I wore my youthful
honors, till some other boy won them from me by greater skill.

Then for running races the palm-leaf wreath is also given;
to win it one must run half a mile forward and back to starting
point without once stopping.

The palm-leaf was given as a prize to the one who could
wrestle the best.   Sometimes fifteen or twenty boys would join
in this sport; and the distinction one boy gained if he could
throw the other fourteen or nineteen times, whichever the case
might be, was something at which to marvel.   The others would

treat him as a king, wait on him and obey his slightest command, till, as I explained before, he lost both the honor and the wreath to some other boy who was victor as he had been.

I could swim like a duck ; could always swim, in fact, for when I was but a very small boy, I was thrown into the water. With dog-like instinct I learned to swim and keep myself afloat, and could live as comfortably in the water as on land. The swimming contests and canoe races were another source of enjoyment to me, as a boy. I was allowed to hunt minor game a very little when I had reached the age of twelve. Some people got a wrong idea here of my age when first allowed to hunt. You know as well as I do that I cannot tell accurately my age.

Boys, under the guidance and direction of some older man, would enter the outskirts of the woods and spend an exciting hour in hunting, most often for the wild goat. Our guide blew a shrill blast on his horn, and we heard his cry of "Ite kear, ite kear," which means "Cease, cease."

Laughing and gamboling like satyrs, dragging the game we had caught after us, we would rally around our guide. We built a large fire ; if we had killed a deer or any animal whose flesh was eatable, we would skin it and throw its carcass on the coals. While the game cooked we would join hands and dance about the fire, whooping and yelling, laughing and poking fun at one another in the illimitable child fashion that is the same the world over. I poke fun at some one else's expense always.

When the deer, or whatever animal it chanced to be, was roasted, we sat around it in a circle with our knives of sharpened wood, and each one helped himself and hacked away at the steaming venison, in a fashion that, if not polite, at least was full of the utmost heartiness and good cheer. For dessert to this impromptu feast, we ate bananas and pineapples that grew luxuriously and spontaneously in the groves around us.

At night we would swing our hammocks, which we always took with us strapped on our backs, up among the trees, and snuggled into them comfortably. The hammocks usually cleared the ground by twenty or thirty feet, and we could go to sleep in comfort, feeling that we were out of reach of any wild animals that might prowl around, attracted by the remains of our feast. As a further precaution against such unwelcome visitors, just before we settled down for the night we built two large fires, one on each side of our encampment. We would lie in our hammocks and call from one to the other till we fell asleep, exhausted by the day's chase.

How often in the dreary, sorrowful days that I have lived since, I have thought of those happy hours, and wished for my native country that is so far, far away! New scenes do not efface the memory of the dear old days; nor do they dim the memories of my mother. I can recall her tender eyes, and her gentle voice, when she drew my brothers and me about her, as lovingly as any white mother could, and talked to us of our father and the respect and duties which we owed to him.

She told us to be true, brave soldiers always, and to die rather than show one trace of fear in battle or in contests of any kind whatsoever. She taught us of our gods. The respect we must show to the Moon; the reverence in which we must hold the sacred crocodiles; and the love and worship we must feel for Carnabah, chief and king of all gods. How our childish eyes would open wide with fear when she told us, in stirring tones, of the penalties dire and awful which we would bring, not only upon ourselves, by disrespect to any of these gods, but also upon the whole tribe.

A terrible plague would fall upon us all—and we would die in horrible suffering, or we would all of us be stricken blind or speechless. A hostile army would invade our land and conquer us, and the Vey people would be slaves for the rest of their lifetime, and their children's children unto the third and fourth generation, would be slaves in their turn. If we showed carelessness in our worship of the Crocodiles they would dry up all the water on the land, and absorb all moisture from the vegetation, so that we would die of thirst. If we ever looked disrespectfully upon any of the festivals in honor of the Moon, no more light should ever be ours. The blackest, gloomiest of night-shades would fall, and would never again be lifted; and in the darkness strange beings and creatures to us invisible would sting and bite and torment us constantly.

Dishonor to Carnabah, God of Heaven, greatest and mightiest of all the gods,—ah! that was visited with such awful punishments that no words could describe them. The vegetation, the air—our own bodies would become ever consuming, yet ever inexhaustive fire. When we spoke flames would issue from our mouths — when we breathed we took hot fire into our burning lungs. Our food would be like hot coals, our drink boiling and seething with heat; and we could not escape this punishment. Wherever we might go it would overtake us and make life a torture and a misery. These are only a few of the many stories which mother told us in connection with our lessons on the gods of our tribe.

Often she told us legends of our tribe, which had been handed down from generation to generation. How the first settler of our tribe was a strong and powerful man, who came with no companion but his wife. She bore him many children; sometimes giving birth to three or four at one time. These children when they came into the world, were full-fledged men and women. At a little over one year of age the females would bear children, and so in this way the territory soon became populated. This first ancestor, Hera, was a very kind, gentle man, and loved his sons and daughters, and taught them of the gods, and of their duties to these. He was of gigantic size and weight; so heavy was he that his foot-prints are yet shown imbedded in the rock, which yielded under his touch, mother said, like so much soft clay. He was so strong that he could shake mountains from their foundation; "and it is from him, Besolow, that you and your people get your great strength." One of Hera's sons was his father's equal in strength and weight, and was a wonderful elephant hunter, thinking nothing of felling that immense animal by one well-directed blow. Then *his* son was famous and powerful, and so on for two or three generations. No stories are told of the kings and princes for the next hundred years. Then comes a story of another· king — a fable in our country similar to the Greek fable of Mercury. This king could fly with amazing swiftness. Far out of reach of the weapons of the foe, he would fly before the army of his own tribe, and ferret out the hiding-place of the enemy, who dreaded the "flying chief" as if he had been a demon.

He fell in love with a certain beautiful woman who belonged to a neighboring tribe, and married her. She knew nothing of his strange power of flight; but discovered him one day in the act of flying away, his arms filled with immense rocks, which he intended dropping, one by one, upon the heads of his enemies, who were unfortunately her own people. She betrayed him to her people. who stole upon him while he was sleeping and took his life. Then was there much lamentation and mourning and weeping among his friends; and "from that day to this, my son," mother said, "there has never been another flying chief born to the people."

A few years afterwards there came to the throne a big, burly king, whose mother had been a lioness, people said; he was very cruel and fiendish. Day by day he would have hundreds of his people brought up before him, and for the delight and pleasure which it afforded him, would have them beheaded by the score. Often four hundred of them would die in this way in one short day; the whole town would take a holiday, to witness this dreadful spectacle. He would have days upon which he tortured, seeming to enjoy this more than when he had the victims killed outright. He would have the eyes gouged out of the heads of some; burnt out of the heads of others with red-hot irons; others would have their lips bitten off by some slave as blood-thirsty as the king who employed him—or perhaps his nose or ears, whichever it might chance to be. Instead of dogs he kept lions and tigers, and quite tame they were; they would lick his hand and fondle about him, recognizing in him one of their kind. When these animals grew hungry he would snatch a babe from the arms of its mother, and throw it to them for their repast, or a young, half-grown boy or girl, even a man or woman, if it so pleased him.

Under his reign the population began to decrease, as you might well imagine, after such wholesale butchery of the people. "One day, after a terrible slaughter and torture of innocent people," said mother, her big eyes very wide open, "there came down to the earth a huge, black cloud; it parted, and, seated on a throne of fire, with blue flames licking him on every side, yet leaving him all unharmed, was the biggest, awfulest looking man or creature! It was hard to make out which he was, or to tell where the man stopped and the animal began. He reached out his long, hideous arms, and a darkness came over all the land as he did so. He took the wicked king Hoodoo into them; and the women could hear his bones being cracked as his lions had so often cracked the bones of their children. In a voice compared to which the loudest thunder is but a whisper, faint and low, he said: 'Come, you wicked one, to Cayanpimbi.' Then the cloud closed and lifted from the earth, and the bad king was never seen again." After mother had finished this story, I looked at the sky with much fear and trembling ; but she said I need not fear : the " cloud-man " never came save to bear off a very cruel king.

This legend used always to have a great effect upon me ; and I would often muse over it for days. When a prisoner was punished in what appeared to me to be a particularly cruel manner, I would look up at the sky with awe-filled eyes to see if there were any signs of the " cloud-man's " coming.

These are only a few of the many stories and legends of my people.

CHAPTER III.

" The bloody act is done,—
The most arch deed of piteous massacre
That ever yet this land was guilty of."
                                        —*Richard III.*

LIFE IN BENDOO.

I WILL tell of the origin of my people, as it was so often told to me by my mother, by the old chiefs of my father's tribe, and once by father himself. It was always of interest to me, and may be of some interest to my readers as well. As my mother used to tell it to me, it ran somewhat in this way: More than two centuries ago, a nomad tribe numbering hundreds of men and women, left Abyssinia, and for many years wandered toward the country west of the central part of Africa, like the Helvetians in the time of Caesar.

At last they arrived at a pleasant territory a little northeast of what is now the Republic of Liberia, and being pleased with the lay of the land concluded to make it their home, and cease their wandering. This country was already occupied by a powerful tribe called the Goolah, but this nomad tribe, called the Vey, were not inclined to change their minds on that account; but in the spirit of conquerors they commanded the Goolah people to take up their abode in some other place. Naturally enough the Goolah king refused to do anything of the kind, whereupon the Vey people began to wage war against the occupants of the land. It was tacitly understood that the strongest tribe, *i. e.*, the victorious one, should possess the land, and evermore hold the conquered tribe as servants—slaves, if they chose to do so. " Might makes right."

For a long time the war raged fiercely, for both tribes were strong and brave. It was not until after a siege of nearly twelve months that the Veys proved victorious and took possession of the territory, which they have held ever since. The Goolahs, humbled and discouraged by the defeat, made no further resistance to their captors, but accepted the subordinate places assigned to them with quiet yet simple obedience. Wishing to bind the conquered people to him, the king of the Vey took in marriage a daughter of the king of the Goolah, and from this union sprang the royal line of kings and princes of Vey, from whom, I am happy and pleased to say, I am descended. Yet some American men do not respect me.

Bendoo, Bendoo, my own, my native town! How often I think of you with tears in my eyes, and with the utmost longing for you in my heart! Would that I could draw a pen picture of my native town as it is; but, alas, I fear—I know, in fact, that I cannot.

Many descriptions have been written and will yet be written to describe African towns and villages; but, after all, I think but a faint idea of these places is conveyed to the mind of the reader, unless he has traveled in some part of the " Dark Continent," or in some other country whose people are but slightly advanced. Scattered over considerable extent of country northwest of Upper Guinea, in the neighborhood of Liberia, lie the various colonies and towns of the Vey tribe. These colonies are very rich in a great many respects. In some of them the ground is so fertile and yielding that cotton will grow continually year after year; and this land will yield not only cotton crops, continually, but also corn, tobacco, and other productions of the torrid zone.

In some of the other colonies vast gold mines are found, and the rivers, in such places, sometimes run yellow with the glittering ore. I have seen such immense quantities of gold-dust at times in my life, that if I told you how much, or compared it to other things that are commoner, and of which you see no lack every day, you would doubt my word. North of the kingdom is situated the town Gorrah; east, Davuma; south, Jalakipalacla, and west Toracora. The Vey or Mandingo tribe is not one and undivided; it is divided into many sub-tribes, who have peculiarities of government, and customs original with themselves, but many of them speak a common language, but are subjects under various kings. But there is a superior king over these kings, and father was, at one time, one of these superior kings. The territory was given the name of Vey after the Vey people who came originally from Abyssinia. Two hundred long years have passed away since my first ancestors left their pleasant or otherwise, home in Abyssinia, for what reason I do not know.   I have heard it said that it was to escape the iron rule of a tyrannical ruler ; but be that as it may, they wandered south and they wandered north before they finally reached and settled upon the lands which they have held ever since.   These first people of our land were named Besolow.   This name signifies " peace," and has been a name much used in our family ever since.   These ancestors, we have every reason to think, were men who possessed some excellent powers—of judgment, justice and mercy.   Under the first king whom they elected, flourishing little hamlets soon sprang into life.   The mines were worked, and the gold obtained made into rude ornaments.   These ornaments are often dug up from the ground by men and boys, and were in my time.   Rude cooking utensils carved out of stone have also been found, and in many cases an attempt at ornamentation has been made upon these, which, taking everything into consideration, was not a very poor attempt.

I have told you about the Goolah tribes whom my people conquered, when they, my people, first came to the territory. So long as this first king who had married the daughter of a Goolah chief, lived, everything moved easily and harmoniously ; the Goolahs were crushed and humbled by their defeat, and fell into the lower places assigned them with sullen obedience. When the king and his queen died, however, they rose to arms, and attempted to oust the territory from the Vey.

Another scene of bloodshed and suffering and torture took place.   I have heard that it was a most cruel war.   Finally, after many a month, the Vey were again victorious, and the Goolah were put back again into the places from which they had attempted to rise by insurrection.   But after this war, and under control of a new king, things did not prosper in Vey lands as they ought to have done.   For a long time everything came to a standstill ; and the people seemed to be retarding and retrograding instead of going forward.   I have often been reminded of that period of my people's history, by a similar one in primeval American history.   I have reference to the Mound-builders, who were such a superior people, and the inferior race who came after them.

Not many years, however, did the Veys remain inactive. It was not their nature.   They are not a lazy people, as a general thing.   Under the reign of another good king, the territory began to improve once more, and from that day to the present day, it has gone on steadily growing better and stronger and more advanced, in a great many respects. Rude ideas of architecture will be found in the minds of a great many,—also ideas, imperfect, perhaps, but still ideas, of farming are possessed by others. The king, of course, is the sovereign; but after all, the voice of the people is heard to some degree through the Council who are called " King's eye," and always sit with the king in matters pertaining to the government. If Christianity was once instilled into their minds and hearts, I think their progress would astonish some of you white folks. I am not saying these things because the Vey happen to be my own people. I say them because I believe my words to be a truism, to which I desire to give expression.

In the centre of our territory is situated the capital, and my birthplace, Bendoo, a really beautiful town, skirted by magnificent forests and clear, sparkling lakes. Situated on a promontory it extends into a large lake called Peso. It is in this Lake Peso where the sacred crocodiles are kept. It is a picturesque sheet of water whose shores are beaten smooth and level by the feet of many pilgrims, from miles around, who come here to offer sacrifices to the gods. In his youth, my uncle had spent four years in Spain, and came home from that country an atheist; therefore he had not succeeded my father long before he had all the sacred crocodiles put to death. He had no respect for those great divinities.

Bendoo occupies a space of a considerable number of miles and has a population of about two thousand souls.

In my father's time it was the seat of trade with the American, English and Dutch traders. Shortly after he ascended the throne, father made a treaty of peace with the Liberian government, and agreed to open commercial relations with them, both of which agreements he kept most faithfully till his death.

Bendoo is built in the form of an octagon, and is completely surrounded by villages. Two fortifications are thrown up to protect it from encroaching tribes or the onslaught of the enemy during war times. The outer fortification is built of mud and hard-wood, and is seventeen or eighteen feet in height. The inner fortification is of less height, and is built of the same materials. In the space between these fortifications, sentinels walk constantly. For greater protection to the town a ditch has been cut all around it, and in some places this ditch is seven or eight feet deep. The walls are pierced by four gates, and stationed at each of these gates a sentinel is always to be found. Every stranger is obliged to prove satisfactorily that he is a friend. Some of them, those who belong to a tribe which boasts a written language, are obliged to show a certificate or pass sentence—*Mo tum dea moo,*—*i. e.*, "We are friends from a distance."

The sentinel calls for another man, who conducts this stranger to the king or his council, before whom he states his business. In this way, the Vey people take the utmost precaution always ; and they are not at all too careful, for some of the tribes in the vicinity are very jealous of our progress, and treacherous as snakes.

There is one long, straight, main road that cuts through the centre of the town, and off this run innumerable small roads and lanes which are extremely narrow and irregular.

The huts of the people are cone-shaped, built of burnt clay and grass, and, except in rare instances, they are not over eighteen feet high. The average door-way is little over twenty-five inches in height and narrow in proportion.

The width and height of the door-ways in this country was something at which I marvelled when first I saw them ; and it seemed very strange that I was not obliged to crawl and wriggle myself through a narrow opening as we are obliged to ; so narrow, in fact, that often a fleshy man or woman would get stuck, not being able to get one way or another, and would cry and pant till some one came to pull them out or push them in.

The framework of the huts is of hard, durable wood, which is daubed over with mud or clay. These huts are wonderfully strong, and so compactly built that often they stand for sixty or seventy years without repair.

The frame-work of the windows is made of bamboo, and there are usually three or four of these windows in each hut.

Father's hut or "palace" was three times as large as the common man's hut, with a much larger door-way, and a finely polished outside door of some beautiful African wood.

In front there was a space spread with leopard skin rugs and straw mats, where visitors could be accommodated, and where the Council sat when they convened to discuss matters of importance pertaining to Vey.

Then surrounding the palace were many courts which contained the huts of father's slaves, and also those of his many wives. In the palace only men-servants were allowed. No woman could approach the building without first obtaining permission, except the woman who holds the key to the storehouse.

The furniture of the common man's house is extremely simple, and very limited. There are two stools for himself and wife, or four, or five, or six stools, depending, of course, upon the number of wives he may happen to possess. A hammock or two will be hung from the ceiling. On the walls, occupying a prominent position, the first objects that meet your eyes are his spear and sword, and one or more skeletons of animals which he has killed. Of these latter he is very proud indeed, and never neglects an opportunity of calling your attention to them. Beside these will hang his war accoutrements, made of the skin of some of the lower animals, unless he be a man of rank, when his garments will be made of tiger skin, well lined with cotton. A few roughly hewn cooking utensils complete the list of the furnishings of the average hut.

In all homes is found the household god, or African Panates, carefully placed in the horn of a ram and glued over, and bought of our medicine men, and which they warrant will ward off any sorrow or misfortune that might chance to be hanging over the family.

Father's hut was more conspicuous than any other in the way of furnishings. As I have said, it was very much larger, and the main floor was portioned off into rooms, by means of curtains of bamboo wood, cut into long, slender strips. There were many more stools, cushioned with skin, stuffed with cotton, and a few rough benches built into the wall; mats of braided straw covered the floor; and in place of cooking articles, the walls fairly bristled with war weapons, and Panates, or household gods.

Large portions of land in the vicinity of father's house were fenced off, and here the domestic animals of our tribe, the ox, the goat, and the cow, were kept safely penned during the night.

North of Bendoo is a deep, dark forest, that is so dense and dark as to be almost impenetrable; while immediately in front of this are immense groves of palms, golden bananas, and big, luscious red oranges, the like of which, in juice or flavor, I have never seen in this country.

Life begins in Bendoo at daybreak ; and when the sun goes down, and night comes on, especially if the night be clear and bright, the people dance and sing about the camp fires till almost midnight. "When the sun goes down all Africa dances."

Father's hut faced directly on the main street, and the huts of his wives were arranged in a circle about it. Father had a hundred wives, or more. Of all his wives my mother was treated with the greatest consideration and respect, because of her high birth, but she was not the favorite or best-loved wife.

Father's favorite wife was a tall, fine Amazonian woman, of much energy and clear-sightedness, named Taradobah.

Taradobah took a great fancy to me, and always treated me with a great deal of kindness and consideration.

My mother held the keys to the storehouse, and doled out, as it suited her, the food and raiment of the other women. She and Taradobah were especially good friends, and there never appeared to be any jealousy between them.

The market-place in Bendoo was a large open space of about sixty or seventy feet. The hum and bustle of the market-place begins to be heard at a very early hour once in three months, for the market for trade between native tribes is opened only four times during the year.

Among the men who gather around the market-place are many buyers, sellers, and idlers.

Here we saw the wealth and riches of the African forests, and mines, and lands ; sweet potatoes, nuts, yams, palm oil, skins, gold dust and ivory, cam-wood, and some finely embroidered mantles of many gay colors ; these were given in exchange for fowls, goats, sheep, oxen, or whatever a buyer had which the seller wanted. In this manner we barter one thing for the other ; the most important and most often employed currency consisted of cloths, gaily colored, cotton, red, blue, and white beads.

Young boys are forbidden to approach within a quarter of a mile of the market-place, and also the place where trade is carried on with the white people. At twelve years of age we are sent away to a forest school, and thus, strange as it may appear, only one boy in a hundred ever sees a white man until he is grown to a man's estate. For the penalty of disobedience, I have explained in a previous chapter. Of course we heard descriptions of them, and I know in my own case, my heart beat very quickly when an old man told me they were white as the lambs were when newly washed. "What hideous-looking, ghastly appearing men they must be!" was my thought. It seemed to me I would rather meet a lion or a gorilla than one of these strange men. The boys used to get together and talk about these strange people, and ask each other what they would do if they should come upon a white man in a forest. "Die of fright," some would say. "Run for my life," another replied. "Kill him," was the response of some others. But no, we would not dare to take his life, for how did we know but that he was a god of some kind, and how dreadful would it be to make an attempt at the life of a supreme one!

On the days when we knew that the white traders were in town, we could think of nothing else; and though we dreaded to, yet we longed to see them, with all a boy's curiosity. We had been forbidden by our fathers to approach that part of the town, and we knew some terrible and harsh penalty would follow if we dared to disobey the parental command.

One day, however, one of the boys, a little fellow of not more than eight years of age, and of a very daring disposition, determined to brave all, and make an attempt, at all hazards, to see a white man, and also the manner of carrying on trade in that mysterious part of the capital that was a sealed book both to him and to us.

We advised him not to attempt any such thing. We told him if he did and was found out, and that it was pretty certain, he would lose his fingers, nose, or worse still, his life. He "pooh-poohed"* the idea; said he'd be very cautious indeed, and started off on his reconnoitering tour, feeling, I've no doubt, very grand indeed, while we waited developments in much excitement and a good deal of trepidation. We soon heard terrific screams and cries, and instinctively knew that it was our daring comrade who had been discovered in his disobedience, and was suffering the consequences. In this case the consequences suffered were the loss of one of the fingers of his right hand, besides a merciless whipping; he was bound hand and foot to a tree, and lashed by two men, with long, thick, leather thongs, till the blood gushed from the wounds as freely as water.

---

* This is a good old African word, used as frequently among my people as it is among people of this country.

Then all of us boys of his own age were summoned before father, and he told us he was going to warn us once again to remain away from the trading markets. The next boy found within a quarter of a mile of it, should lose his life. "Wander," he said, "where you will, in other parts of the town, or in the forests, but keep away from the markets. No mercy shall be shown to the next disobedient boy or girl."

Our curiosity concerning the white man was, as you may well imagine, considerably dampened, and remembering the fate of our companion, we shunned the markets as we would have shunned an evil spirit.

It has often been asked me : " How is it that you had never seen a white man till you came to the mission, when your father, right in the town where you were, carried on such extensive commercial relations with Caucasians ? " I always answer this question as I have done above. The southern part of the town is devoted to nothing else but trade ; but the white man dare not cross a certain prescribed limit of land, or he, like the native boy, may lose his life. So though the white man may be very near the African boy, he is also very far away ; he might as well be in America, or England, as far as the black Vey boy is concerned.

Father was very anxious that some of his sons should learn to speak the English tongue, so that they could help him in his business, as interpreters. He employed about two thousand men, but only one in every hundred could speak anything but the native tongue. He himself knew only a few English words and phrases. Then he determined, instead of sending me to the usual African school, that he would send me to the mission at Cape Mount, on the coast. When I learned of his intentions I was in despair. What ! be sent among those terrible men, whose skin was white, like newly washed lambs, whose hair was light, like the sun ! No, no, no ! I would rather die many, many times over. I went to mother and wept, and begged her to intercede for me with father. I went to Taradobah, also, and pleaded with her to do the same ; i. e., intercede for me with my father. I would be such a good boy, I said ; I would never disobey in the slightest particular ; I would strive very hard to become a brave and fearless warrior and hunter ; I would offer many, many sacrifices to the gods, if they would only save me from the miserable fate of being sent among the dreaded white people.

What horrible kind of a country was it, I asked them, where those people lived? What would they do with me when they got me there? Might it not be Cayanpimbi (hell)? I pleaded so earnestly that both mother and Taradobah consented to use all their influence with father to have him change his decision. Of all mother's children, I am glad to think that I was her favorite, that she loved me best. She was very averse to my going; for if I went she said she knew she'd never see me again.

She had many animals killed and offered to the Moon and Carnabah, beseeching them to permit her son to remain in Bendoo.

Just at this time there was to be a grand festival, if I may so call it, in honor of the Sacred Crocodiles, and I distinctly remember the thrilling story as it came from the lips of my mother, I myself not being present, a boy, as I was, not being allowed at the sacrifice.

Five years had elapsed since the last one had taken place, and preparations on a larger scale were made for this one. The town took on a gala appearance. The women plaited feathers and leaves in their hair, bedecked their persons with all the beads and jewelry they owned, and joined the others in roasting the carcasses of animals which men and boys were busily engaged in killing and dragging from the woods.

The musicians were out in full force, with their clappers, and horns, and drums,— the air was filled with the melody(?) of hunting and war songs. Medicine-men, in their best toggery, mumbled to themselves as they moved about the town, with airs of importance. Why should they not be self-conscious? Were they not, on this great day, to perform the sacred rites and ceremonies in honor of the gods?

People from other parts of the country — from the north, south, east, and the west — began to arrive in Bendoo by the hundreds. There were blind and lame, old and young, sick and well—all constantly arriving, till it seemed that there would not be space in which to accommodate them all.

Yes, Bendoo at this time must have resembled Jerusalem just before the feast of the passover, when it was filled with pilgrims who were bent upon seeing and speaking to Christ; or like the "Jews' Wailing Place" in Jerusalem, where it is the custom to this day, and has been for many centuries, for the

Jews to approach the " temple of their fathers " and moan and pray beside it.

Right here, my dear reader, I want to say a few words. Do not get the idea that such a great concourse of people would come together for the purpose of a sacrifice in my behalf alone. I want to speak particularly of this, because in my former edition a good many people were misled in regard to the occasioning of this sacrifice. Through haste in this place in copying and cutting the MSS. written to fill a book of three hundred pages, but cut to some over one hundred, there occurred, naturally enough, some errors, which in this edition I shall aim to correct, and this concerning the sacrifice to the crocodiles is one of them. This was the story that was put in the former edition as real fact, and that I was an eye-witness. This is false. I could not have been an eye-witness, on account of my age. This blunder was made by the party who cut the number of pages from three hundred to some over one hundred.

This is a great festival that takes place in Bendoo once in every five years, and it chanced that the day for observing it dawned during my troubles in regard to being sent away to the mission. Hoping this is now clear to my charitable reader, I shall resume my story.

When all the people had arrived who were likely to come, a blast from many hundred ivory horns announced to the waiting natives that the ceremonies were about to begin. The scene was a striking one. The people — men and women rushed down to the shores of the lake, pushing and scrambling for a standing-place in a way that was dangerous alike to life and limb.

My mother told me, before going, that she should offer prayers to the gods to prevent my father from sending me away, and also that it was a very fortunate thing for me that the sacrifices were to be offered at this time, as she believed that the crocodiles would listen to and grant the prayers of a loving mother for her son.

I will tell this story, with some comments, as nearly as I remember it told to me.

The hour for the sacrifice was at hand. Suddenly a deep silence fell over all. Fifty or more medicine-men were approaching the shore. They wore long, floating, white robes, and looked very sober and solemn indeed.

About a dozen feet from the shore could be seen the red, hungry eyes of a half-hundred crocodiles. Their great, gaping, slimy mouths were opened greedily, as if they were eager for the expected feast. The low, drawling voices of the medicine-men were heard for a half hour or more in an unintelligible harangue; then through the crowd there pushed their way twenty-five slave women with their naked babes in their arms. At this point the musicians began to play upon their instruments—the dancers began to execute some wild, fantastic dances —the singers began to howl, for no other word expresses it— the voices of the medicine-men grew louder and shriller, and amid all this, the spectators with many a prayer and promise to the gods fell upon their knees and rocked themselves to and fro as though in mortal anguish; and all the while the gleaming eyes of the crocodiles seemed to dilate and grow larger, and their capacious, horrible mouths seemed to look more greedy and expectant. The only quiet ones in the crowd were the slave mothers and their babes. To look upon them was a sight never to be forgotten. The tears were silently dropping from their eyes as they bent over their little babes, who were cooing and throwing up their little chubby hands into the air, happily unconscious of the horrible fate awaiting them. The mothers quickly and quietly brushed away the tears, however, for if caught in the act of weeping for their babes, their own life, in all probability, would have paid the penalty.

These babes were to be offered as sacrifices to the crocodiles; and what greater honor could be conferred upon a slave-woman than to be asked to offer her child as a sacrifice to the gods? After the priests had finished their long harangue, they took the babes from their mothers' arms, one by one, and annointed their naked little bodies with fragrant oils and salves; and then the mothers, in their supposed joy at the proceedings, were expected to dance and caper about, and sing a propitiatory song to the gods, in which they fervently hoped that the sacrifice would please them, and be sweet, tender, and toothsome. How dreadful it was! What a strain it must have been upon those mothers to have pretended joy and pleasure when, in reality, they must have been wretched and miserable beyond expression. Bravely they hid their feelings and danced about, throwing their arms into the air, and screaming shrilly, perhaps in this way venting their grief, as one after another of their infants were cast into the waters of the lake, to the waiting, greedy animals. The crowd watched with fascinated eyes the little black bodies disappear into the cavernous mouths of the crocodiles, leaving a long stain of crimson blood dyeing the waters of the lake. Distinctly on shore could be heard the monsters as they cracked the bones of the unfortunate babes, whose pitiful cries of pain might well have touched a heart of iron; and all the time the mothers danced and sang merrily. At last it was over, and only the eager eyes and cruel heads of the monsters looking for more prey to devour, and the blood-reddened waters bathing the shores, remained to tell of the scene just enacted.

Though I was young, and accustomed to terrible scenes, yet when this scene was pictured to me, I remember that I felt a throb of something very like pity, as I thought of those poor women who had sacrificed the lives of their babes, but as I write about it now, man grown as I am, it comes to my mind with all its fearful significance, I cannot keep back the tears. May the one just, kind, and merciful God free my native land from a custom so horrible! May He endow me with such strength and grace that I shall be able to help in abolishing a system so cruel and debased.

May the Divine Spirit take possession of the hearts of many men and women, till they feel called upon to go out into my land as missionaries, teaching the misguided people of Him who is the embodiment of love and tenderness and gentleness; and asks not the babe of its mother, nor the son of his father, nor the wife of her husband, in horrible sacrifice; but asks only for the love and consecration of the human heart to himself, and the enlargement and enlightenment of the soul in Jesus Christ, our dear Lord and Saviour. Africa has been well explored and lakes and rivers geographically placed, but it will be many a year before all the dark portions of Africa will be warmed into life by the sun of Christianity.

It happened that mother and Taradobah had influence enough with father to cause him to change his mind in regard to sending me to the mission; and mother told me how grateful I should be to the gods who had favored me, and answered my supplications. I *was* very grateful and happy indeed, to escape from the terrible, I knew not what, fate awaiting me, as I believed, in the mysterious land of the white man.

One of my brothers, Geesah, however, a fine-looking boy, much older than I was, by the advice of a trader was sent to England, to a preparatory school. I believe he proved himself wonderfully quick and capable, and it was not long before he was able to enter Oxford or some European College, which he did. How much I pitied him, and condoled with him upon his fate; and how much I admired his seeming carelessness of what awaited him in the "strange land," and his courage in attempting it. On the morning of his departure I said adieu to him with tears in my eyes, for I believed that I would never see him in life again, and I was most fond of him.

His life and the lives of the whole family will be written during my college life. The name of the book will be, "The House of the Black Princes."

After that, several times, father threatened to send me to the mission—word synonymous, in my childish mind, with every terrible and unknown horror of all kinds, descriptions, and degrees. Each time mother and Taradobah persuaded him to alter his decision; but I began to live in constant dread of being sent away, and was overjoyed when, along with four hundred boys of my own age, *i. e.*, eleven or twelve years of age, it was agreed that I should be sent away to an isolated African school, from which I could not return till I was old enough to fight, and to understand the war and law principles of my tribe.

CHAPTER IV.

"The poorest education that teaches self-control, is better than the best that neglects it."—*Herting*.

HUNTING SCENE.

"The blood more stirs to rouse a lion
Than to start a hare!"
                    —*Shakespeare*.

AFRICAN SCHOOL LIFE.

To this African school I went with the utmost thankfulness and joy. I was to be with my own people, and not with a strange, dreaded kind of whom I knew nothing. I was to continue my friendship with my young companions for many years more. How happy I was! The school was on a peninsula, far away from all human habitation. I would have no intercourse with my mother for many years. I would have no food sent me, and unless I could kill game, would be hungry many times; our teachers had perfect and unlimited control over us,—they could treat us as they were pleased, and no one would interfere. But I cared not for all these things; be my treatment ever so cruel and hard, I could bear it so long as it came from the hands of my own people, and not from the much-dreaded, often-threatened whites.

It was a long, hard tramp of many days from Bendoo to the school, but I did not care for that. I rejoiced to cut my way through deep, tangled jungles and brush that might have daunted a strong man; for every step I took forward was I not leaving that hated mission farther and farther behind?

It makes me smile now when I look back at that time, and remember what an unceasing, powerful fear of the white people had taken possession of my mind and heart.

We trudged along then right merrily, rather glorying in the cuts and bruises we received, and the aching weariness which we felt in our limbs. This was the first step toward becoming a brave and famous chief and a courageous hunter ; and to become these was, I may truly say, the height of my ambition.

At night, when we swung our hammocks well up among the trees, I would lie and watch the red gleam of the camp fires, and dream wild, imaginative dreams of my future life. How I should become a king like my father, and subdue all the tribes around me ; nay, why not subdue all Africa? Africa was a very, very large and powerful country, father said ; then if it was once in my power, what should prevent me from capturing or annihilating *white people?* Ah ! thought that made me hide my face in my hands, and cower down in my hammock, and shudder at the sleepy cry of a parrot over my head, who was disturbed by the light of our camp-fires.

Gradually the thoughts of fear would leave me, and I would look up and resume my dreams. Africa once in my possession, I would offer, oh ! so many hundreds and hundreds of sacrifices to the different gods, who would favor me specially because of them. I would build shrines of solid gold in honor of Carnabah, and six sacrifices should be offered on them every day. I should have all the wives I wished, and they should be tall and beautiful like my mother and Taradobah.

Ah, the battles I should fight ! I closed my eyes then, and lived over those battles in imagination, till my senses wandered and I fell asleep.

We breakfasted off some fish or game we had caught, quaffed the water of a lake, and then resumed our march. At last, footsore and weary, we arrived at the peninsula (wrongly stated island in my first edition) where we were to remain for several years. We swam from the shore of the mainland to the peninsula. As soon as I landed on it I set out on a voyage of discovery, accompanied by several of my mates. There were on it no human beings but ourselves.

At this place, in the first edition, a mistake occurred. In the original MSS. the distance was written in Persian parasangs, and the copyist in copying it, wrote it miles. She was not acquainted with Xenophon's Anabasis. Fifteen parasangs were given, but fifteen was omitted and parasangs left out, and miles put in ; it was simply a chirographical mistake. Fifteen parasangs would be about forty-five miles. You see here that I tried to show my classical tastes, and got into trouble. To resume my story : I heard the sound of the horn calling us together, and went hastily to the edge of the shore upon which we had landed. With us were our teachers, about fifty of them, large, strong, stern and valiant old warriors, whom father had considered worthy and had appointed to teach us.

When I reached the shore I found them gathered in a group, talking earnestly among themselves. They commanded us to remain quiet, and we were still as a country churchyard. Not a sound was heard while Zolusingbe talked to us. He told us we had come there for three things. (1) To learn the code of law of our tribe. (2) To learn the art of fighting and war tactics. (3) To learn to show proper reverence to our gods, and be disciplined for the place in the army which we all desired to fill. If we were well-meaning and diligent we would be well treated, and consequently would be happy : but if we were lazy or disobedient, the same punishments would await us for both as had awaited us in Bendoo.

The other teachers followed with like addresses ; then we were permitted to rove whither we would, till the sound of Zolusingbe's horn should call us to the place from which the sound proceeded.

It was very pleasant and exciting to explore the depths of a forest that was new to us ; and what could be more interesting a place than a luxuriant tropical forest, with its spontaneous growth of delicious fruits, its nests of eggs, the minor game, the pools alive with fish of various kinds, and the magnificent trees often reaching a circumference of twelve feet, more or less. It was quite a feat to climb to the very topmost point of such a tree ; but we little fellows could climb like monkeys, and scaled gigantic trees with the ease of one, jumping from limb to limb with a recklessness that might have cost us our lives ; but lives were seldom lost in this way.

The next day our duties began. Into our hands, such eager hands, too, as they were, were placed a bow and arrow. We were told that we had permission to shoot any lesser game that might cross our paths. What airs we gave ourselves ! and how proudly we set off on our first real hunting expedition ! Imagine a white boy given a weapon, and sent into the deep, dangerous forest to hunt, as a matter-of-course. It was in our school, as the alphabet is in yours, the rudiment, the foundation of an education, or what was considered by my people as an education.

We hunted all day. I had been luckier than the others, and at the shrill horn signal, that in the quiet reigning about us, when the boys' yells were lulled, could be heard for more than a mile away, I came back to the old men, dragging after me more game than any one of the other boys. For this, Zolusingbe patted me upon the head, and said I was a smart boy. I felt as proud as a king; and though very tired after my day's hunt, was very happy, and ate some of the game, when cooked, with a relish.

Zolusingbe was an old, grizzled war veteran, and from the beginning my favorite among all the others. He took much interest in me from the first, and showed me many favors; not because I was a king's son, for rank counts nothing in our school; but because he really liked me as much as I did him.

He had a class numbering about fifty boys, of which I was pleased to be a member. For several hours every morning we would gather about him, and he would show us how to throw spears, and to use the sword in the most skillful manner; how to use the bow and arrow with ease; and with a gun he had as an object, he explained to us as best he could, that form of weapon, which, however, he called treacherous, and advised us to leave it alone. I think he took more pains in teaching us how to use our native weapon, the spear, and was very proud of us when we began to handle it with some degree of proficiency. Then in the afternoon we would hunt, and grave displeasure would be visited upon us if we did not come back with as much game as he thought we ought to have. After supper, he would teach us war dances and songs; we would practice target-shooting or spear-throwing; and then, tired out, we were glad to crawl into our hammocks and fall fast asleep. And there was no let up on this *régime*—it was the same day after day.

We soon found that we had not come to that spot for mere play and amusement; but if we ever wanted to get through, we were obliged to work hard and earnestly, and practice with our weapons as often and as long as we could. It was hard. Often I grew so tired from practicing spear-throwing, that I almost wished to die; but Zolusingbe and the other old chiefs had no mercy on us. and when we showed the least sign of weariness, called us lazy, and weak women-boys. Though tired and sleepy, as we often were, our exercises and practicing went on the same as ever.

A portion of our meals was always offered to the gods before we ate, and sometimes a whole carcass would be offered intact; at home we also offered part of our meal to the Panates. Each boy in turn would be obliged to conduct the sacrificial ceremonies, and dance and clap and sing the praises of the gods till Zolusingbe gave him permission to stop. We used to dread this, for the chiefs would grow very angry with us if we didn't follow their teachings of these rites to the letter.

One year passed in this way; and though it was a hard, taxing one, as I look back upon it I realize that it was far from being an unhappy one to me. Our year equals about 200 days.

Those dear, happy days of my boyhood!

At the beginning of the second year we had mock battles. Half of the boys, about two hundred, would form one tribe, and the other half would represent another and hostile one. The woods were cleared by us, with the help of the men, and a certain number of acres of land was divided off from that adjoining. This land was the supposed territory of one half the boys, and the hostile tribe was desirous of obtaining it, and were going to use harsh means to get it into their possession. The captain of each detachment was selected by lot, and the boy who was a coward was not allowed to have lots cast for him; only a boy of stamina and character can be voted for as captain.

The mock battle often became one of terrible reality, and the boys fought and punched and bit one another, and laboring under the stress of an excited imagination that made the fictitious seem truth, would separate only when some of the men tore them apart. If the attacking party drove the others off the land, it was considered a distinguished honor, and the boys would be praised and feasted, much to the chagrin and disgust of the other half, who would sulk and scowl sometimes for days. If the attacking parties were repulsed six times, then the victory belonged to the other side, and it was their turn to become jubilant, while the other boys went about in seeming disgrace and discomfort.

You can imagine these mimic wars were very exciting, and in them we put into practice, one by one, the war tactics of our tribe, as fast as they were taught us. The first war tactic we learned was the manner in which to besiege a town. We learned that nearly all African towns were strongly fortified; sometimes having, like our own town, *two* fortifications, an inner and an outer one, besides a deep, wide ditch. In such a case, when the enemy could fire upon us while we were crossing the ditch or scaling the wall, especially if they were a tribe who used powder and shot, and could kill many of us before we could enter their town, the better way would be to build a wall about the town, and within the wall build little houses or towers, cut the enemy off from the water which supplied the town, and keep them shut up in it till their provisions are gone, and they are nearly dying of thirst. Then, nine cases out of every ten, when greatly moved by hunger or thirst, they will surrender; if not, they are too weak to fight well; and a determined attack upon their barricades, and storming of their walls, will conquer them. If you fail, then retreat; and when the enemy is not looking for you, when it is thundering, raining, or so dark that your moving figures cannot be seen, then creep upon them and renew the attack. Again, it is extremely likely that you will take the town.

This was the first tactic that we learned and put into practice; surrounding the boys and keeping them without food for many days, till through sheer hunger they were glad to surrender and own themselves defeated. However, sometimes they would drive us backward, and keep us off till some of the men declared they had gained the day. I say "us," because I was usually in the attacking party.

Second tactic we learned after having mastered the first, was the following: "Arrange your men," said Zolusingbe, speaking as if we were all going to be generals in our time, "four or five miles from the town in a circle, then let a small posse of men attack the town, pretend to grow fearful and flee. The enemy, in chasing them, will get in between your men, who will close in upon them before they realize what is taking place, and so surprise them that their defeat is almost certain."

This, too, we put into practice exactly as Zolusingbe described it; and I remember how he called us all about him that night, and told us that we were brave boys, and got his ideas very quickly and well. Ah, how proud we were then! For my own part I seemed to be treading on air; and the dreams of glory that came to me in my hammock that evening were more mighty and grand than ever before. There were other worlds besides Africa, Zolusingbe told us; why should I not conquer them? Though I didn't know about Alexander at the time, surely my youthful spirit was very much like Alexander's in its ambitions.

Over and over again we applied these war principles; and it was not till toward the close of the third year that the third tactic was taught to us; and the men called it taking the town by stealth, or stealing the town.

A man is sent into the town under the guise of a friend, bearing a friendly message, telling them he has come from a district or tribe from which he has not. He asks for a place to rest, telling them he is weary. Then, at night, he steals upon the sentinel at one of the gates, and disposes of him, if he can (and only men who are likely to be successful on such an undertaking are sent), and opens the gates for the army outside, who steal in upon the town, and take possession of its supplies, while its inhabitants are sleeping They give the war-cry then: "Ticihiah arcu, ticihiah doobur," meaning, "We are here, we are here." Then we begin the siege. Each man of the attacking party must take a house, and is supposed to conquer its inhabitants. The contest may last for twenty-four hours,— a hand-to-hand fight,—and, of course, victory is a fickle jade, crowning sometimes one tribe and then another. Like school-girls' love—she soon finds another fellow. I can tell from my own experience.

Two years of our time passed; and we considered ourselves as proficient in the use of the different weapons as it was possible for any one to be. This was very boy-like; we had come to that point in our lives when we thought we knew it all, and what we didn't know wasn't worth knowing. The men looked on and smiled, and indulged and encouraged this self-conceit we had, instead of trying to smother it. I think they thought that conceit was the salt of character; without a little of it, men didn't amount to very much, after all. But our pretensions to excellence and strength were put to the test in the following fashion: the boys were made to stand side by side, directly opposite the same number of chiefs. One boy at a time came forward and wrestled with the chief. If the chief put the boy down very easily then he was declared weak, and could not be advanced with his training, but began again on some of the principles he had been over; but if the chief had some difficulty in putting down a boy, the boy was promoted, and this continued down the line till each boy's strength was tested in this way. Fortunately, or so I considered it, I not only was *not* downed, but came within an inch of tripping Zolusingbe, with whom I was wrestling. My strength—and for a boy, I was wonderfully strong—pleased and delighted him, and he sent a message to my father to the effect that I was his best and favorite pupil. Father sent word back that he was delighted with my progress and very proud of me; and I'll wager he was not half as proud of me as I was of myself. After our strength had been tried, our endurance was tested in a very cruel way. We were made to stand back to a chief, who, with a stout, tough piece of leather, with thorns stuck jaggedly into it, gave us a prescribed number of lashes. Those of us who bore the treatment without flinching, were declared brave boys who could go on; those who winced, or moaned, or cried out were dubbed cowards, and never afterwards looked upon with proper respect or affection. Poor fellows! I do not wonder that some of them begged for mercy, for many of us will bear to our graves the marks of the blows received in school, given when our enduring powers were tested. My own back was pitifully sore for many days; but I made no sign, and practiced as long and as faithfully as ever at target-shooting, running, and jumping. Zolusingbe was watching me narrowly, I knew; and I would have died, one, yes, a hundred deaths, sooner than show to him that I suffered one particle of pain from my scabbed, aching back. Yet only God knows what I did suffer; and instead of bright dreams of future conquest coming to me that night in my hammock, I lay on my face and bit my lips till the blood came, to keep back the groans that rose to my lips, while the scalding tears poured down, unheeded, over my cheeks. I was only a little fellow, and though I despised myself for my tears, I pitied myself, and they would flow. In the morning, however, brave as the Spartan boy of whom we read in Grecian history, I was up and at my duties, with a smile upon my lips.

Here, for the first time, Zolusingbe grew vexed and displeased with me. I have told you of the gun which he had. It always hung in his hut of tree leaves and bamboo which the chiefs had built for their use. I was, and had always been, very anxious to handle this gun, and see if I could fire it off as Zolusingbe had done for my amusement on rare occasions. One day he was going to the mainland with another chief to hunt. I watched the canoe that held him out of sight, then stealthily and like a thief, I crept into his hut, got possession of the gun, ran to the shore, and jumping into a canoe, paddled swiftly out into the middle of the lake. As I paddled along about three miles beyond the peninsula I overtook a canoe full of men evidently of a strange tribe. The canoe was loaded with oranges and bananas. Seeing me, a boy alone in a canoe, they concluded they would have some fun at my expense, and began to call back to me in a tongue, that, without being exactly familiar, was intelligible, extremely insulting words. I felt my blood begin to boil with rage, and called back to them that they had better be silent or they would suffer the penalty; they laughed me to scorn, and continued their insulting expressions. I saw a large water-bird flying low before their canoe, and, in an authoritative way, demanded them to cease paddling, and not scare the bird. They kept on, answering my command with a contemptuous laugh. While their laugh was yet sounding I brought the gun to my shoulder and took deliberate aim at the tallest paddler. Terrified at sight of a gun, which by many African men, was looked upon as you would the devil himself, they, like one man, leaped from the canoe overboard, just as I fired it off.

When they rose to the surface they were not out of gun shot, and were swimming for the shore as rapidly as they could. I took their canoe in tow, and paddled back to the peninsula flushed and elated with victory. I found Zolusingbe waiting for me. His face was ominous as a thunder-cloud, and I trembled when I heard the sound of his voice, which was like that of father Zeus. Where, he asked me, where had I been; and how came I by his gun? When out on the lake in canoes, we were not allowed to go out of sight of the peninsula, and I had been three miles out of sight. I told him briefly. I think if he had liked me less, he would instantly have put me to death, which he was at liberty to do, and which would have keenly disgraced the name of Besolow. But he loved me, he expected great things of me, so he spared my life, upon my firm promise that I would never, as long as I lived, disobey a superior. As it was, I had the wounds on my sore back opened afresh, and was tied to a post hand and foot for three days, without food and drink. I cannot describe the state of my feelings. Miserable, wretched, —I wanted to die. What was there to live for now?

Zolusingbe would never care for me more. But Zolusingbe was magnanimous, and he took me to his heart again; and from the minute he cut me down from the post, weak, and sore, and fainting, and fed me on cocoanut milk, till the day I left him forever, he never referred to my one serious misdemeanor while at school. You must not let the word school mislead you, for these are things that were done in jungles.

CHAPTER V.

THE GORILLA.

"Il n'est de serpent ni de monstre odieux.
Qui par l'art imité ne puisse plaire aux yeux."
—Boileau.

"Cowards die many times before their deaths;
The valiant never taste of death but once."
—Julius Cæsar.

HUNTING SCENE—ANIMALS.

FOR six months we practiced using the weapons of our tribe, and reviewed the war tactics, which I have explained to you besides many more too numerous to mention. We went on several tiger hunts with the men, and watched them and their methods of disposing of those savage beasts.

The sight of the prey, brought to bay in a jungle, as he turned upon us with his flashing, fiery eyes, showing his teeth in a fierce grin, and lashing his tail backward and forward rapidly in his rage, fired my blood, and excited me as nothing else had ever done; and I begged Zolusingbe to let me dispatch him.

"You!" he said, in amazement, looking down upon me from his lofty height, with fine scorn—"you!"

"Yes," I answered, boldly, grasping my spear more firmly. "I am sure that I can kill him."

With a laugh, he waved me to a place behind him, and I had the satisfaction of seeing the foaming beast killed by one of the oldest chiefs.

One of the boys skinned the animal; and the process of removing the skin neatly from the animals was an act that we also learned while at school, beginning first to practice upon the smaller animals. The skin was a very handsome one,— the handsomest, I think, that I ever saw,—and when it was well dried and dressed it was sent home to my father, with the compliments of him who had killed the beast.

We were taken on several such hunting expeditions, to get used to the ways and tricks of the ferocious inhabitants of woods and forests; but, as the men said, that manner of hunting was mere play, and that the following year, when we were stronger and better fitted for the work, they would show us what a real African hunt meant. One day they set us at work digging near the centre of the deep forest. We dug a pitfall under their direction, seventy or eighty feet long, twenty-five or thirty feet wide, and about eight feet deep. It was not easy work, toiling for many days under the hot, broiling African sun, but we dared make no complaint; and then, besides, some pleasure was derived from the thought that we were making preparations for, as Zolusingbe said, "a real African hunt," in which the bravest of us were to take part. At least, this was an impetus for me to work. Every spadeful of snarled, rooty earth I cast one side, I would think, was a-helping on the time when I should really stand a truly developed hunter. Just as when we have a long walk before us, we fix our eyes on a certain object ahead and say, "Now, when I reach that, I shall have so far finished my journey," and continue in this way till the journey is over.

The pitfall we dug was capable of holding a great number of animals. At each end of the pit we laid the trunks of big trees, and also placed them about the sides; in this way forming around it a kind of fence. Then, under the dictation of the old men,—practical hunters they were, too,—we built, in a more or less workmanlike manner, two fences of triangular shape, the pit being the apex. These fences we built of stones, tree-trunks and branches. These fences were about a mile in length, and at the extremities, I think, quite a mile apart.

It was a month and over before we had completed our work, but when finished at length we surveyed our architectural attempt with infinite pride and pleasure, and I for one forgot that I was weary and that my arms ached.

One fair, warm day, Zolusingbe put our spears into our hands, and told us that we would that day put our knowledge of them into practice in a manner that would doubtless cost many of us our lives. He charged us to be careful, and gave us many directions, too many to enumerate. We were a goodly number, about two hundred of us, and were separated into divisions, each division commanded by one of the old chiefs.

We turned out and surrounded the forest as well as we could. Then by all sorts of stratagems and tricks we tried to decoy the animals into the space between the fences.   It was many hours before we had succeeded in accomplishing this, for the animals were very wary, and doubled on their tracks and ran into ambush in a manner that was very exasperating.   As for me, I could scarcely contain myself, I was so excited.

Only my fear of Zolusingbe, and that he would send me back to the encampment if I was too eager, saved me from attacking the animals before they were gotten between the fences.   At last, however, many of them were worried into the space intended for them, and we formed a phalanx across the broad opening.   At a word of command from the chief in charge we advanced towards the pit in large numbers, thus driving the animals forward.

A heterogeneous collection enough they were too, consisting of zebras, antelope, deer, and wild-cats, and many smaller animals.

In the narrow part of the triangle the sides of the fence were built very strong, so that the frantic efforts of the animals to escape by pressing their bodies against the sides could be of no avail.   At length they entered, a heterogeneous mass, the narrowest part of the triangle, and the pit gaped open, a grave, before them.

At a word from the chief, we charged forward in a furious manner, yelling and brandishing our weapons, and terrified the animals to such an extent that they rushed onward blinded with fear, and fell headlong, one after another, into the pit.   It was of no use for the foremost ones to hold back, as doubtless many of them did, for the pushing, rushing mass behind would force them in.   In a very brief space of time the pit was quite full of groaning, fighting, growling, dead, and dying animals. By running over the bodies of the other animals, when the pit had become full, some of the beasts escaped, others turned and endeavored to break through the ranks of our advancing party, but they were quickly disposed of.   Their bold dash for the life and liberty so sweet to them, availed them naught.

I shall never forget the moment when I first came up within a few yards of the pitfall.   In it the animals growled and raged and squirmed and fought each other, in a manner that might have caused the stoutest heart to fail, and grow sick with fear; but fear I did not know at that time, nor does an African native on the hunt ever know, there is such an emotion.

The unfortunate animals were interlocked; some lay on their backs as they had fallen, with their feet kicking frantically in the air; of others all that could be seen was a head, with a pair of wild, affrighted eyes, rolling rapidly from side to side. A tail was all that was visible of some, a foreleg of another, and a narrow piece of flank of others again.

It was a horrible sight, and I shudder now as I think of that bloody, snaky, writhing mass of flesh and blood, but at the time I thought it was a fine, grand sight; and my face was wreathed with smiles, my heart was full of satisfaction, when the old chief told us to advance to the edge of the pit and dispose of them. He told us to be cautious; but I think little caution was observed by any of us, as we began to despatch the animals in a more or less scientific way. We drew out the dead and wounded, and disposed of those beneath, and went on in this manner till all were dead or rendered too helpless to attack us. They were not all destroyed, however, without many of the boys losing their lives; for those animals fought for their lives, even those of them who were naturally timid, with a persistency and fierceness at once wonderful and pitiful to see. One of the chiefs lost his footing and fell in among them, and before we could help him he was torn almost to pieces. I regret to say that once again I am obliged to call the attention of my kind reader to a mistake made in the former edition, in this place, by the party who cut the book down. The book spoke of a tiger being caught in the pit along with other animals, and said that the unfortunate man described in the foregoing sentence was torn to pieces by it. This was not true. There was no tiger in the pit. Whenever a tiger was trapped in a hunting excursion of this kind, we boys were quick to allow him to escape through our circle. We didn't often trap one on the peninsula, but did quite frequently when we hunted on the mainland, and of course we hunted indiscriminately on both places.

After we had havocked all the game, we set to work, and, reeking with the blood of our slain victims, bulit immense bonfires, in preparation of a feast we were to enjoy. We cooked some of the animals that were eatable, and partook of their flesh greedily, for we were hungry after our long day's hunt. After that we howled, and danced, and sang the hunting songs we had been taught, at the very tops of our voices.

We offered several carcasses to the gods, and those that were valuable for their hide we skinned, under the direction of Zolusingbe and the rest of the men.

Loaded with all the game we could carry, we wended our way towards the shore and our encampment, still yelling out our hunting songs and rejoicing.

We were summoned up before our teachers, who commended some of us specially for our bravery and the facility with which we handled our weapons. I was one of those to be commended for courage, and ah, what a moment of triumph that was ! And how the hammock dream that night grew in magnitude, till the world, were it fifty times as large as it is, would be none too large to hold the Utopian castles I built.

They were sad dreams, too, for I was inclined to mourn for my young companions who had met their death that day. I wondered if they were at Igenie or at Cayanpimbi. I wished that I were able to offer many offerings to the gods in their behalf.

I spoke to Zolusingbe the next day of my grief for them, and he was very angry with me. "If you are a woman," he said, "you had better return to Bendoo, and confine yourself to womanly duties, and give up all thoughts of becoming a warrior and a hunter; for silly regrets have no place in the hearts of such."

It must have been amusing to see the airs we boys gave ourselves for many days after our first hunt; and indeed we were fond of strutting. When the hunt was an old story, as it soon became, Zolusingbe was fond of telling me that I was a hero, because I was more agile and proficient than all the others. Zolusingbe favored me, perhaps. However, I know I loved to hunt, and put into it all my heart and strength.

Some days we went out to hunt on the mainland especially for larger game. Then the pit was filled in, so as not to be so deep; and then we set out to snare the elephant and buffalo, whose weight prevented them from leaping from the pit when once in it. Hunting for elephants is done by the most experienced of hunters. We boys were mere onlookers, so that by observation we might acquire knowledge of hunting.

These larger animals were havocked in a similar manner, with still greater danger to the hunter; for an enraged elephant is indeed a mighty enemy, and swings around its trunk in a manner that causes the attacking party to keep at a very civil distance. It used to take us a long time to kill an elephant, especially where we had no other weapon but the spear. They were so immense that sometimes it was a long time before the spear would strike a vulnerable spot; and we didn't try hard to hit it in a vital spot, for we rather enjoyed to see it suffer, and to see, also, the frightful rage that every fresh blow lashed it into. So it suffers long and most cruelly before it finally receives the blow that takes away its noble life.

We used to consider the elephant a rare prize when we were so fortunate as to entrap one, because of its tusks, out of which, as I dare say you are very well aware, some of the very finest ivory in the world is made. When we had collected a goodly number of tusks, they were sent to Bendoo to be traded off for rum or tobacco. Then, the elephant's flesh was eaten by us with much enjoyment.

These pitfalls which we dug in the woods for hunting purposes were a source of much anxiety to travelers, who never knew when they would be precipitated into one of them at the imminent risk of life and limb; and especially dangerous are they at night.

They often become overgrown with vines and tangled creeping grasses, and one does not know that he is in the vicinity of them till he goes crashing through the vines and lands at the bottom of the pit.

I remember how the chiefs taught us boys to tell when a pit was near us, by observing a certain hollow sound in the ground under foot; but it was very difficult to catch this nice little distinction in sound, and only the trained and the practiced ear of some old hunter could do so.

All our time was now spent in hunting game. All day long, for week after week, we were constantly testing the principles taught us. The enthusiasm of the men fired us to do brave deeds, and prove that the pupil was worthy of his teacher, and each teacher was especially anxious that the boys under his particular charge should do as well as lay in their power. They were eager to hunt as we were, and we had always living examples of courage and valor. I think, excepting war, there is nothing a Vey man loves so much as he does the chase.

Whether we hunted alone or in companies,—and we did so in the latter way more often,—but no matter in what way we hunted, no matter for what we hunted, large game or small game, we entered into it with a thorough heartiness and enjoyment worthy of a better cause. Such a wonderful variety of game, too, as we stirred up in that thick, moist, luxuriant forest's depths! I think a greater variety was found there than could be found in any other country in the world.

There were antelopes from the largest to the smallest kind, zebras with their handsome striped coats, giraffes, lions, and elephants. Every lake and river teemed with fierce, strange animals; even the trees seemed alive with them, and every jungle was occupied by them.

As I grew older I particularly liked to hunt the antelope. There was somehow or other a zest about it which was missing in the hunt for all other animals. They were very sharp and wary, and had a curious way of lying all huddled together in such a manner that they resembled nothing so much, from a little distance, as a pile of dried grass and withered leaves. So much did they resemble these things that I have known even the keen, practiced eye of Zolusingbe to be deceived by them.

They ran very fleetly, and seemed to have a really wonderful agility in dodging the spear, and bow and arrow. I used to say that they ran in between the arrows, for they were of slender build.

I was never easily discouraged, but persevered till I brought down the animal; for after a certain limit the animal grew very tired, always, often lying down in sheer exhaustion, permitting us to come up and dispatch it without a sign.

It is an animal that can live for a long time without water. With a wonderful instinct, it used to lead me through the hottest and dryest parts of the country, in which there would be no springs or water; and often I would become so thirsty that I would be obliged to return to Zolusingbe empty-handed.

I was taught to regard the horns of the antelope with special reverence, for they were the receptacle in which were placed the panates and talismans, and we boys regarded them with great admiration, as the men scraped and polished them. They are also useful in trade. I believe they bring a good price in this country, as well as in my own.

The antelope is very gentle and timid, but when brought to bay will turn on its pursuer, to fight for life.

I remember once how one of them turned suddenly on me, when I had hedged it in in such a manner that it could not escape. It lowered its head very nearly to the ground, and directed its horns towards me, and charged upon me, endeavoring to lift me on its horns and gore me through and through. These horns were sharp as knives, pointed as needles, and if the animal had succeeded in lifting me upon them, I shouldn't be here to tell the tale. I moved to the right as it came rapidly forward, and as it passed me by, planted a spear in its side. It fell, moaned in a very human way, and after wagging its head to and fro, it gave a final gasp, rolled over and died.

Thinking over all the narrow escapes I had while in that school, I think God must have meant to save my life because he had some work for me to do.

I have told you how the elephant wended his mighty way through the depths of the wood, in the thick jungles, under which lay hidden venomous reptiles, which seemed ready and waiting always to spring upon the unthinking and unwary one. As I lay in my hammock at night I often heard the roar of majestic lions, within gun-shot. Tigers lay all day couchant upon the tree-limbs.

The forest was not a pleasant place nor a safe place in which to travel; but for myself, who was a born lover of adventure and excitement, there could be no place like it in all the world.

Gaily plumaged birds, whose tinted feathers far outrivaled the hues of the rainbow in beauty and variety of color, flew from tree to tree. These birds were very handsome and gorgeous, and there were many sweet songsters among them, some of which would rival the nightingale.

The parrot, for which I always had a strong admiration, was as common as the bird you call the English sparrow; and the monkey as common as a cat, as they jabbered and chattered all day long in their funny, noisy way; and often have I been awakened in the morning by one of these mischievous little fellows throwing wild plums down upon my head. I wonder now why it was they didn't crack my head open; as it was, such a mode of waking me from my slumbers made my head pretty sore and did not improve my temper.

CHAPTER VI.

RETURN TO BENDOO.

" Such joy ambition finds."
—*Milton.*

" All praised the legend more or less;
Some thought it better, and some worse
Than other legends of the past."
—*Tales of a Wayside Inn.*

THE GORILLA.—A GORILLA STORY.

IN the densest part of the forest the dreaded gorilla lived. It may well have been dreaded. From the top of a high tree I saw one about this time, and my heart beat most rapidly at the sight. This one was over six feet in height, and apparently very strong, for it went crashing its way through the thick undergrowth of shrubs and bushes as if they had been so much grass. I was all alone and unarmed, and I knew if it spied me my life was over. I scarcely seemed to breathe; but in some way it seemed to realize that another presence besides its own was in the neighborhood, and paused and struck a listening attitude. Then it slowly advanced in my direction, till it stood directly under the tree where I was. I called upon the gods to save me, and my prayer ran somewhat in this fashion: "Hear thou me, O Silver Bow! If my grandfather and grandmother, if my father and mother, have at any time offered unto thee the carcasses of fat animals, burnt for thee the fat thigh of many bulls and rams; if they have at any time done anything for thee gracefully, oh, then hear me, Carnabah, and avert from me this direful destruction which is threatening me." I cannot tell you all the offers I made to them of coming sacrifices. I begged them to send Zolusingbe or some of the men to my rescue; but he did not discover my presence, and after a little while disappeared into the thickest of the jungle. I was not long in scrambling down off the tree and making my way to the camp, where I related the story, embellishing it till some of the boys got the impression, I think, that I had had a single-handed contest with Mr. Gorilla, and with one hand strangled him with all the ease in the world.

One of the chiefs promised to tell us a gorilla story that had been handed down to us from our ancestors of a hundred years ago; some night, he said, when we had been hunting hard all day, and were resting about the camp-fires. A gorilla grows from five to six feet, and walks erect. Its arms when outspread measure from seven to nine feet. You can imagine what a formidable animal it is to meet when unarmed, or indeed at any time. They are as strong, if not stronger, than the lion, and seem to have a special hatred for the human beings they so much resemble. Their claws are sharp as razors, and some of the claws are from two to two and a-half inches long; and when the animal is excited it seems that the claws attain a greater length.

It never gives a man time to think or collect his senses, but in most cases springs upon him at once, and almost crushes him to death in its ferocious embrace. I remember a boy of the school—a tall, straight, well-formed youth,—the son of one of father's prime councillors. He was a brave, fearless boy, and he and I were together a great deal, running races, canoe-ing, fishing, and hunting side by side. He, like myself, had most ambitious dreams and aspirations; and as we trotted along together, or performed our varied duties, we would talk over the lives we had pictured to ourselves with much delight and eagerness. Poor Hingbe!

One morning his teacher sent him into the forest alone to cut rosewood for spear-handles. He was very neat about wood-cutting, and was often sent when they wanted nice wood to procure it. The picture of him as he stood beneath the trees, with the golden sunshine, sifted through the thickly interlaced tree-boughs, falling over his smooth, shining, naked body, that was held so proudly erect, is printed indelibly upon my mind; his earnest eyes shining, a smile on his face, and his long, sharp spear gleaming in his hand as he listened to his teacher's directions. "Come here, Besolow," he said to me, just before starting, and willingly enough I obeyed him. With a smile he held out his hand and I put mine into it. This was a custom that was in vogue with us, and it did not strike me as being very strange in him. He held my hand for some time. "I wish you were going, Besolow," he said; "good-bye." "Good-bye, Hingbe," I answered, and I watched his sun-flecked, brown body till, singing a gay hunting song, he plunged into the thick woods, and was lost to sight.

That day I spent out on the lake in my canoe fishing. When I went home at sunset and asked for my companion, they told me that he had not yet returned.

We danced that night, and sang in honor of the moon, who was just showing a fine, silver rim of her face in the sky. All through the noise and hurly-burly—for noise was always, and is now, a necessary accompaniment to festivities of all kinds—I missed Hingbe, and wondered why he did not return. He had not come back when we retired for the night. His hammock hung next to mine, and I lay and watched it in the moonlight, as it swung idly backward and forward in the faint wind that' stirred the tree branches ever so faintly. Somehow I couldn't sleep for thinking of him, and I think I must have had a presentiment of what was coming.

The next day he did not return, nor the next; on the fourth day a search party was organized to seek for him, and I was chosen as one of its number. All day we sought for him everywhere, giving the peculiar call by which we made our whereabouts known to each other while separated in the forests.

It was I who at last heard a strange, weak response coming from the deepest part of the forest at my right. The others did not hear it, but, guided by me, we made our way to the spot from which the faint cry had proceeded; and oh, how I sicken at the thoughts this narrative calls to mind! We found Hingbe, or what was left of him, in the lair of a gorilla.

The animal, fiercest of its kind, sprang upon us, but was soon overpowered by numbers, and dispatched with haste; and then we gave our attention to our companion, who was lying on a pile of leaves, and, though half eaten, was, God help him, not yet dead. I went up to him, and savage though I was at the time, and used to sickening scenes of bloodshed of all kinds, I am not ashamed to say that I trembled with emotion and pity as I bent over the prostrate form of the boy, who, only a few days before, had bidden me good-bye so gaily, and had left me so strong and handsome and full of life.

All the fingers of his hands had been bitten off, as had been also his toes; one foot was partly devoured; his nose was gone, and both his ears, and his eyes had been dug from their sockets; and, horrid thought—he still lived and suffered, as his moans foretold, lacerated over and over!

"Hingbe," I said, in a voice very soft and tender with pity, and a civilized brother could not have felt more pity in his heart than I did in mine for him.

Hingbe was taken away by the chiefs, and I never saw him again. In my first edition I am made to dispatch him myself; this was not true, and the misstatement came as other errors came, to which I have already called the reader's attention.

It is a common thing when a man is suffering for him to request his friends to kill him, and thus put him out of his misery. We regard the man who makes such a request as an honorable soul, and the one who does the deed as both an honorable man and a kind friend. It is deemed better to stop suffering even with death than to let it continue when there is no possibility of recovery. The fatal blow is given without a tremor, for we know the afflicted one is better out of his pain, and then, a savage man has not that keen perception of what is cruel and wrong that a civilized man has.

It was many weeks before the sorrow caused by his sad fate left my breast. It seemed to me no soul departing this life ever left behind a more sincere mourner; my companion gone, even this savage life seemed robbed of much of its light and joy. Poor Hingbe! I sigh even now as I think about him.

We dragged the gorilla's carcass home with us, and told the remainder of the party of Hingbe's melancholy fate. "Dread the gorilla," said Zolusingbe, "more than you do any other animal in the world. It is exceedingly cruel. It loves to torture its victims. In its hideous, crushing arms it will bear them to its lair, and with a cry that sounds peculiarly human will call its mate and young about them. The unfortunate man or woman who has fallen into the gorilla's power is gradually destroyed, and sometimes has the misery of seeing his limbs torn from his body."

A person rescued from a gorilla is, in nine cases out of ten, literally half destroyed. Rescuing parties must always number fifty or sixty men, at least, for one gorilla is equal to any twenty men ; and when attacked, by a strange call, attracts others of its kind to its help ; and they fight in a manner that causes many a one to lose his life.

After Hingbe's fate, I dreaded meeting the gorilla as I had dreaded—yes, and did still dread—meeting a white man. The two were synonymous horrors to my mind and imagination.

While the excitement concerning Hingbe was still rife in our hearts, an old, dried up, weazened chief told us the promised gorilla story one night, as we all rested about the campfires. It was one known to all the members of my tribe, and was believed in firmly, as well.

I sat with my arms about my legs, which were huddled up till they met my chin, and listened to his words with the greatest eagerness. As he talked he would look around him in a nervous manner, and then, with a shiver, would stir the fire at which he sat into a brighter blaze, and hold over the flames his long claws, that had, indeed, lost all seeming semblance to hands. This chief claimed to be over one hundred and twenty-five years of age. In appearance, he certainly looked it ; but his strength and endurance were both those of a man of fifty.

"Over a hundred years ago," said Keetsie, "a certain king of Vey had a very beautiful wife ; she was his favorite wife, and he loved her better than all the others. She was faithful to him, and seemed to return his affections. One day she was missing from the town, and could be found nowhere. It was learned that, at an early hour in the morning, one of the men had seen what he supposed to be a huge gorilla, on the edge of the forest adjoining the town. There was no doubt, then, either in the mind of the king or the minds of his people, that the loved one, the favorite one, had been taken away by the gorilla, and was even at the time suffering tortures.

"A body of men, as well armed and equipped as though they were going to war, started for the woods, which they searched carefully for many days without avail ; and, at last, upon finding no trace of her whereabouts, they were obliged to give up the search, and come home without her. The king mourned for her many months, but at last became reconciled to what was inevitable.

"Two years afterwards, when he and his men were returning from a hunting expedition through the thick forest, they came accidently upon somebody's hut—whose, at the time, they were much puzzled to know. It was of mud, and quite well and strongly built.

"They marvelled at finding a human habitation in the very heart of a dense forest such as this one was. They entered it, and one of them who claimed to do so, was the old chief who was telling the story. He stirred the fire into a brisker blaze, and looked behind him in a manner that made us huddle closer to him. The hut, he said, contained two stools: and on the walls hung cooking utensils similar to their own.

"As they were making these examinations and wondering among themselves who could be the occupant of this lonely abode, they were startled by a shrill, queer cry not far away— a cry that chilled the blood in their veins. It was the cry of a gorilla. 'Oho, oho, oho, yahco, yahco, yahco'; and the very leaves from the trees fell. There were but few of them, the old chief said, throwing on the fire several extra logs, but they were quite well armed. They drew together as they passed out, and alert and in readiness for battle, awaited developments.

"An immense male gorilla came in sight, with his arms loaded with wild cocoanuts. At sight of his uninvited guests, the animal stopped for a moment, amazed; and then, with a howl of rage, began to throw the hard cocoanuts into the midst of the men, with quick, unerring aim, and with a force that was terrific enough to knock some of the men senseless.

" He was the largest gorilla that I ever saw," said Keetsie; while the others of us scarcely dared look to the right or left, and started nervously every time a monkey leaped from one bough to another, or a parrot muttered sleepily to its mate. " He was ten feet in height, boys; and his muscles and sinews stood out like iron, and were as hard as iron, I know. His face was very human, the features standing out clearly and distinctly, and being well formed. As soon as he saw the necessity for help, he began to call for his mates, throwing the wild cocoanuts all the time, and keeping well out of spear-throw as he did so.

"Others, how many and how powerful we did not know, would soon put in an appearance in answer to his call. We were only a handful of men, and could not hope to cope successfully with many such as the one before us. Still we resolved to make a fight for it, and drew closer together, when, lo, boys! from out the woods, robed in skins, and wearing a wild, strange expression upon her face, came a woman.

"When she looked directly at us, we saw that it was no other than the king's favorite wife, who had disappeared two years before. For an instant she seemed half ashamed when she recognized us, but only for a moment; then she appeared to recover her self-possession, and going boldly to the side of the raging animal, put both arms about him and actually talked to him in a quick, hurried way. What she said we could not hear; but he seemed to understand, and became very calm, dropping the wild cocoanuts, one by one, as she talked. He put his great arms—I know they never measured less, when outspread, than ten or eleven feet—he put those horrid arms about her quite lovingly, and ceased calling for help.

" She gestured in our direction a good deal, and by that we knew she was conveying to him something concerning us. He nodded his head sagely for a few times; then she turned to us, and told us that in the woods back of us there was an army of gorillas, who might appear at any moment in answer to the call of their mate. We might go in peace and safety because we were her friends; but she advised us, if we valued our lives, to get out of that vicinity as quickly as we could.

"The king asked her if she did not want him to come back and rescue her from the arms of such an inhuman husband; but she answered 'No!' quite sharply, and said she was happy and contented as she was.

" In spite of her words, however, the king did come with many of his warriors, to take her back to the town, to her people; but we found the hut deserted and destroyed, and the woman and gorilla gone, and we never saw them afterwards; but old men have said they have seen, and I won't say that I have not also, the wraith of a terrible ghostly figure, half gorilla and half woman, who appears to some member of the tribe just before a misfortune of some kind is to befall it."

I can't describe the low, weird voice, the strange, fearful eyes, and the trembling and thrilling gestures, of Keetsie as he told us this tale. I for one was glad when it was finished, and I didn't sleep much that night. When I did, I dreamt of the woman who was part gorilla and part human, and awoke with a start, to strain my eyes through the thick gloom, and to start at every sound made in the trees upon which my hammock was swung.

This gorilla story of Keetsie's, and Hingbe's death at the hands of one, haunted me constantly; and every time I went into the woods, I expected to be borne off and devoured.

Of course this story of Keetsie's does not sound very probable to me now; but at the time I heard it I accepted it in the utmost good faith.

True or not, the fact remains that this animal is a terrible foe, and my people are frightened of it, and they are frightened of nothing else. Courage and a Vey heart are synonymous in all things besides.

I was very lonely at times; as lonely and mother-sick as any civilized boy could have been. I missed Hingbe. There was no other to whom I could talk of my ambitions, and of the conquests I intended to make in the years to come. He had always understood and sympathized with me, and others would only laugh, and call me "silly boy," so I spent much of my time in hunting alone or with Zolusingbe, who encouraged all my self-conceit. He said I ought to be proud. Was I not the son of a powerful king? and did I not know more of hunting tactics than all the other boys put together? He was proud of me, he said. He was going to write* to my father that he had a son who was worthy of all his affections; but all Zolusingbe's words of consolation could not cheer me. I seemed to have a presentiment, and a strong one, for the second time in my life, that some misfortune was to befall me.

I used to creep away by myself and make offerings of small game to the moon, and ask her favor and implore her love, in a way, though not for worlds would I have let Zolusingbe or any of the others know of this longing.

How I wished to be a man, and go out to fight. That was my ambition now—to fight a real battle. Hunting had become somewhat trite and matter-of-fact, and I longed for novelty.

Alas, the change was to come soon enough ! How little I thought then of the vicissitudes I would suffer, and how little I then grasped or thought of the One who led me into the Light Divine, and has filled my life with a peace that does indeed "pass all understanding;" that proves to me now that, bar-

*The Vey man has hieroglyphics as letters.

barian and all as I was at that time, I had a nature that was intensely religious. I wonder if the Eternal God took to himself that spiritual uplifting of the naked savage boy.

I began to suffer much physical pain, caused by ulcers, of a very painful description, on the sole of the foot. This was owing to an annoying worm, we called the "jigger," becoming imbedded in the flesh of my foot.

I had taken the utmost precaution, too, to prevent this worm from finding its way into my flesh; but, in spite of the leather sandals I wore, it did get into my flesh; and the consequence was the painful ulcers I have told you about. The worms were very common in the forests, and are, indeed, very common in Bendoo. I could not walk at all. During my affliction Zolusingbe was kindness personified; and was very gentle and tender with me, bathing my aching feet with cool water, and lancing them, when occasion demanded, and binding them up in palm leaves. When I had recovered from the ulcers, a few of the other boys and myself were formed into a class to study the Code of Law and principles of government of our tribe.

CHAPTER VII.

"Our life was but a battle and a march."

—Goethe.

" Things thought unlikely, e'en impossible,
Experience often shows us to be true."

—Shakespeare.

RETURN TO BENDOO.

I was very restless now, and longed to return to my native town. I often spoke to Zolusingbe, and asked him when I would be allowed to return. " Patience, patience," he would answer ; " there are many years before you yet, my boy, and these moments which you wish may come to an end may be the very happiest in your life."

As is apt to be the case with young people, I doubted his words. Hingbe gone, and the mysterious—once mysterious— hunting of animals a common drudgery, no longer tinged with the delights of novelty, this aimless life seemed monotonous enough, and I wished more and more for active life.

About this time, under Zolusingbe's direction, I began the study of what is known as the "Code of Law" of our tribe. I spent much time over this, studying every part of it minutely and thoroughly.

Now, I do not deny but there are many men of our tribe who are degraded and lazy enough—there are such among all nations in the world ; but if they are ignorant on many things, there is one thing they all *do* understand, and that is the " Code of Law" of their tribe. It was simple enough. Among the many, I might almost say hundreds of principles which it sets forth, the following are considered the most important :—

I. The duties and responsibilities that were incumbent upon all warriors during war times, and the best way of meeting these duties and responsibilities, and the penalty which followed the failure to do so.

II. The different modes of punishing prisoners, and when it is deemed advisable, of killing them.

III. Kindness shown by another tribe is to be answered invariably by kindness; but hostility is to be met with a fierce, unyielding spirit, and punished without mercy.

IV. That we should never kill a woman, no matter if she be free or bound, and no child under ten years of age. No cruelties or tortures should ever be imposed upon women captives.

V. If a nobleman of high birth be caught, his head might be taken off, if it so pleased his captors, but he never could be sold as a slave.

Oh! the weary, weary days I spent, after I had mastered the code. At last Zolusingbe brought me one morning the glad news for which I had been longing. "Rejoice now, Besolow," said he; "the time for which you have been longing and waiting has come at last."

"What do you mean?" I eagerly inquired. "A war is about to be waged between your father and King Cobbar, of Lake Tchad, over a portion of land they both claim; and to-day a messenger arrived from your father, asking if there were any of the boys here who were capable of fighting for him."

"O Zolusingbe!" I cried, starting to my feet and seizing his hard hand, and bowing over it as if it were the hand of a god. "O friend, my teacher, permit me to go back with you; I will try to distinguish myself; I will fight, ah, how I will fight! I will prove that I am not a coward; they will never say that you made a mistake in sending Besolow to them."

Zolusingbe smiled a little. "How eager you are to leave here. Going to battle, boy, is not the glorious thing which you picture it. It is hard work. There are nine chances to one that you'll fail; for not only have you to dread the onslaught of the enemy, but there is much to dread in the way of jealousy and intrigue among the men of your own party."

"I know all that, Zolusingbe; you have often told me of that, but I do not care for all these things; only give me a chance to fight, and I will prove to you and the whole world that I am not afraid to die. I will make every one admire me so much that they will never think of being jealous." I went on, with all a boy's egotism, and my heart swelled at the thought of really and indeed participating in a genuine war.

I believe I got down on my knees to him, and finally prostrated myself at his feet, in a way we have when wishing to be very humble, beat up the dust in great clouds with my hands and feet. "Get up, Besolow," said the old man; "I intend to send you and a few others back to Bendoo to-morrow." For half a mile I think my exultant cries of joy and pleasure might have been heard; and I danced into the air, and whirled about till the old chief, the trees, and the sky, became a maze before my eyes. I wondered how the other boys, who were to return with me, could take the news so calmly. I looked at them in amazement, as they listened quietly to Zolusingbe's directions for our trip to-morrow. They in their turn, I have no doubt, were equally astonished at my glee in the thought, and my noisy manner of showing it. It was of no use, I *could not* keep still. I climbed trees, ran around in a circle, ran down to the shore and plunged into the lake waters, over and over again; but it was of no use, as I could neither climb, run or jump off my unusual exuberance of spirits.

I often think of that time when I see the young American boy's delight, as the school days draw to a close, and he sees a long, full, useful life before him. True, I had spent many happy hours in this forest school, but it was not liberty, the dearest thing on earth to me.

That night I didn't sleep at all; I lay quietly in my hammock with my arms clasped over my head, and gave myself up to my thoughts. I thought much of the dead Hingbe, and wished with all my heart that he were here to share my happiness. I saw the moon, one of my favorite gods, peep out from behind a cloud, and I thanked her for her kindness in moving my father to send for me, and promised her no end of thank-offerings when the battle was over.

The next morning I was up before any of the rest. As I looked at the hammocks and the sleeping boys in them, I was puzzled to know how they could sleep so soundly on such a morning.

I ran down to the shore and plunged into the lake for the last time, and then sat on the shore, basking like a salamander in the rays of the sun, that grew hotter and hotter every moment.

Zolusingbe and I built a blazing fire on the shore, and cooked some small fish; and by the time these were cooked, the boys had crawled out of the hammocks and were ready for something to eat.

My people are moderately polite, having a set of rules to govern in such matters—more of which I will explain by and by. At the common board, however, etiquette is not observed to any great extent. The boys squatted about the food that had just been cooked, and each one carved for himself, evidently believing in that old maxim, "Fingers were made before forks."

The meal finished, the chiefs called us about them for the last time, and presented each of us with a garment of tiger skin and a shield of hard, polished wood. Until this time, and since our birth, we had been more or less perfectly nude. They talked to us at length, then bade us good-bye, and prayed that the favor of the gods might go with us.

Without a single regret I started on the march. It seemed to me that I walked on air, and marvelled again at the indifference shown by the others. We grew very tired, however, after a brisk onward march of days, through swamp, and brake, and immense vine-hung forests, and a considerable degree of my enthusiasm had burnt itself out. We were all glad when the chiefs called a halt. Then one of our number lost his life. I do not think I have mentioned tree-snakes to you before, and a word about them here might prove somewhat interesting. They are a long, thin snake, about the color of the bark of a tree, upon the branches of which it clings. It is not readily seen, and before its victim, who is all unconsciously walking beneath the tree, realizes that it is in his vicinity, it makes a flying leap through the air, and quick almost as it takes to tell of it, buries its fangs in the top of his head. Before he can dispose of it or drag it away, it nearly always has stung him so badly that death will result after much agony; for the poison of the snake's tongue goes through the veins and arteries like lightning, causing them to swell to an enormous size, and turns the blood to a deep-blue color.

To protect ourselves from this fate, we wore on the top of our heads a flat kind of hat made of bamboo and lined with cotton. In some parts of the woods there are more of these reptiles than in others. In the woods where we had been at school there were not many of them, but in that part of the woods where we called the first halt on our homeward journey, they were very numerous.

This young man went off to hunt by himself, and left behind him his garment and hat. An hour later he came back swelled to almost double his natural size, with his eyes bulging out of his head. It was unnecessary to inquire what the trouble was ; he had been stung by a tree-snake. That night after horrible sufferings he died, and we buried him in the woods, laying beside him his garment and spear, shield and sandals, besides the freshly killed carcass of a hyena, and a drinking-cup and a sword.

That was the only thing of any moment that happened to us on the march. When nearly at Bendoo we met a party of one hundred or more boys, under the guidance of their chiefs, on their way to the school. With what a lofty air did we greet them ! In it was all the superiority of our condition, of senior greeting freshmen. We asked the chiefs about the state of things in the town, and they informed us that my father was very busy making preparations for war. The soldiers were being drilled, and the gods were being propitiated, and everybody was more or less excited.

Finally, one day at sunrise, we arrived in the town. Our arrival was greeted with a tremendous roll of drums, and the wild native dancers pranced all the way before us singing songs of welcome. How strange everything looked—the many conical huts, the smooth main road ! A breakfast of roast game, and bananas and yams was spread on the ground for us, and we fell to and ate with a great relish, finishing off with a mouthful or two of whiskey all around, which I confess I did not like, and which almost strangled me with its strength and fire.

As I played about with the other boys, word came from father that he wished to see me. With an elated heart I followed the messenger towards his palace. He was sitting in the courtyard, and squatted all about him were the ten men who comprised the council. They presented quite a striking effect. Father sat or squatted on a high eminence ; he wore a flowing whit undergarment, with tunic of bright scarlet. My father was a fine-looking man, tall and broad, and these robes set off his dark, smooth skin to advantage. The councilors wore long cloaks of purple and red, knotted at their right shoulders, which, when they sat, spread out over the ground behind them like trains.

Father beckoned me to come towards him, which I did, prostrating myself at his feet and throwing great handfuls of dust over my body, to show my respect and reverence for him.

"Rise," he said in a very kind voice, and I obeyed him. "Beso-low," he said, "I hear very good accounts of you while away at school. Zolusingbe has told me that you are a brave boy, and know not the name of fear. You are my son, and I am proud of you. You and the boys who have returned with you shall go with me to battle. I hope I may not be disappointed in you."

When he had finished I again prostrated myself in the dust, and told him that I would do everything in my power to prevent him from being disappointed in me.

"It is well," he said ; "you may remain here for awhile, and witness the transactions that take place."

With my heart very nearly bursting with pride and delight at this unlooked-for condescension on the part of my father, I took a seat on a grassy knoll a little to his left, which was covered with a gay rug in which a great deal of yellow and red predominated, helping in its small way toward the pictur-esqueness of the scene. Then my father addressed himself to his councilors, who seemed to be in deep quandary,—that is, if one could draw any inference from their downcast eyes, their tightly clasped hands, and their thick brows knitted into a thoughtful frown. It appeared that they were considering a perplexing question concerning the coming war, and could not come to a satisfactory conclusion about it.

They had been sitting for three or four hours, and were no nearer to a conclusion that pleased them than they had been at the beginning of the meeting. At last one of the men, the chief councilor, rose, and making a low obeisance to father (for every time a man addressed the council he did so, similar to the Greek customs in the Agora), said : " There is only one thing left for us to do. We must be granted greater wisdom before we can decide on the matter before us ; and you know, King Carttom, what will give us that wisdom." He seated himself after this speech, and all the other council-ors looked more ominous than ever.

Father nodded, and seemed to be in deep thought. "Are you sure," he said, "that wisdom will come in no other way?"

"Yes, yes," chorused the men ; "it is the only thing that will bring wisdom to us now." I wondered to myself what in the world this mysterious wisdom-giving power could be, and why the men seemed so eager to have it and father loth to grant, but I was not destined to find out. Father rose, looking every inch a king, with his long, floating, handsome robes falling gracefully about his majestic form. "Be it granted unto you," he said slowly; "wisdom you must have." Then he called me to him, laid his hand upon my head for an instant, and dismissed me. I went rather reluctantly. Afterwards, when I asked Zolusingbe to explain these mysterious proceedings, he shook his head and told me that he dared not divulge the workings of the council; indeed, as I learned later, it was a secret society, whose members, or those cognizant of its inner movements, dared not speak of them on pain of death.

When I met my mother she was very glad to see me, and called me her "*din bella, din bella*"—(good, brave boy). She spoke to me of the war, told me to be careful, and not to be too daring and thus lose my life. She took me with her to see Taradobah, who embraced me as warmly, and seemed as glad to see me as my own mother had been.

I sat on one of the stools and chatted with her about my future for a long time. She broached the subject of the Mission to me, and said now that I had become such a large boy, I ought to entertain some thought of going there. It would be such an excellent thing to learn the English language. Because, by and by—who knew?—I might be in my father's place, and knowing their tongue, could conduct so much better the business with the traders. The thought of the white people and going among them did not frighten me as dreadfully as it had done some time before; but it was not a pleasant thought to entertain, and I told Taradobah that I would rather die than go. "I do not want to learn to speak English," I said; "if I should ever stand in my father's position, I could hire interpreters, as he had done."

"But how would you know that your affairs are going as you would have them? How would you know but that some of these interpreters would cheat you?"

"Like father, I would soon learn a few business terms and phrases, so that I could carry on the most important of my affairs myself."

"It would be a good thing for you, Besolow, to understand *everything* that was going on. There is a certain trader from Hamburg, Brumm by name, agent for H. C. Woermann & Co., who is continually advising your father to send some of his sons to the Mission, and I think your father intends sending you."

"Taradobah," I said, "not now; not before the war. That would be too cruel."

She smiled. "I do not know," she replied, "but I *think* it will be after this battle. So prepare yourself. Do not look upon it, Besolow, as anything to be dreaded; it will be a fine thing for you." I shook my head. "I have a son whom I am going to send. He is very eager and anxious to go; and he will probably never occupy such a high position as your mother's sons will."

All the old fears came back to me when I left Taradobah. I had no heart to play. The boys and girls were jumping rope, and target-shooting, and called out, ·"Come, Besolow; come and join us." But I shook my head moodily. It seemed to be fated that I should be sent away from my people to the whites. "After the battle was over," Taradobah said. The battle will be over in a few months, and then—what would come to me? Was this to be the fulfillment of all my ambitious, lofty dreams— to go among an unknown people, to an unknown land, and learn to chatter in their language? What did I care about their language? Nothing in the world. I went to mother again with my grievances, and with her hand upon my head she promised to do all in her power to prevent my going. She was not at all in sympathy with father about my going away. I have told you her reasons; she loved me, and felt that if I left her to go among the white people she would never see me again.

A little comforted by her assurance of help, I went out and joined in the games. Busy scenes began to be enacted. We boys who had just returned from school, were drilled from day to day by an old and experienced chief, and reviewed all the war tactics and principles in which we had been instructed while away. Father often reviewed his troops, and made any suggestions which occurred to his mind, though he never drilled us.

MY DEAR BESOLOW: It has been some time since I have written you to an extent. This will be somewhat lengthy, and in it I take pleasure in acknowledging the receipt of your favor of the 7th February last, in which you again state the fact that you desire to have and maintain a University for the education of your people at Bendoo.

You desire me to be a trustee as well as adviser. I shall place myself in that attitude to the University, and shall do all in my power to render the project a success. Besides, it is my intention to take a trip up to Bendoo at an early date, as I have never been there before, and survey the place to see whether for all parts of the Republic it can be desirable and accessible to students. The only work to be done here with respect to the execution of your plans, is simply this: that you get the land by gift, or otherwise—say about five hundred acres—erect your buildings, etc., and then I shall assist you in regard to the charter of incorporation, etc., etc. I fully endorse your views with respect to the education of our people. The only drawback to Africa is the ignorance of the masses. I was always favorably impressed with our aboriginal brethren, and deem them capable of becoming part of the body politic of the Republic, but the leaders, "self-styled," still reject them. This prospective University, however, will be, in my opinion, a potent factor in accomplishing the desirable. Had our fathers, upon their first landing, married and intermarried among the aborigines, to-day we would have had healthy, vigorous, and virtuous wives; numerically more than what are now.

I long to see you home again, my boy. You must write and state when you are coming. Remember, Besolow, for truth and honesty stand up, and as long as you work in that groove. in me you will have a warm friend and brother. Before your return home I would like very much for you to visit Baltimore, my second home. Go to Sarah Ann Street, and call for Miss Annie E. Chew; she is my cousin; she will receive you kindly. Use my name to her and it will be well. Again, Besolow, if you go to Baltimore, find out from my cousin where Mrs. Fannie M. Clair, formerly Fannie M. Walker, is. She is my adopted sister, and a perfect lady. She formerly lived at Division Street, Baltimore, but I am informed she has moved to Virginia; and then, Besolow, if you find this young lady, mention me to her as her adopted brother, and she will receive you warmly. At all events, find out her address,—somewhere in Alexandria, Virginia,—for I desire to write her. Tender her my profoundest brotherly love. Induce these young women to come to Liberia, and others of rank and importance elsewhere. Since home I have been, difficulties and trials dire I have had, yet have surmounted them. So courage, my boy. Take care of yourself. Write soon. While I have to remain,

Your true friend,   JOHNS.*

*Thos. A. Johns, Attorney-at-Law, former confidential bookkeeper for Henrick Mulher & Co., Rotterdam, Holland.

CHAPTER VIII.

"Where's the coward that would not dare
To fight for such a band?"   —*Marmion.*

THE WAR.

The busy days preceding the war began to dwindle down to the time for march, until at length the day dawned upon which we were to leave Bendoo. Two hours before the sun rose, the long, rumbling roll of kettle-drums resounded throughout the town, and called us together.

The chiefs surveyed the different regiments, and we quickly fell into line.

The chiefs wore the following dress: First came a shirt of flesh-colored, almost pink cotton, which descended to the knees, and over this was a tunic of tiger skin. Directly over the breast was a protector, made of solid silver. In the very center of these breast-shields is a little compartment, in which is placed, and locked in securely, the god of defense. No one but the medicine man knows of what this god is made, and it costs anywhere from twenty-five to fifty dollars.

About one hundred dollars' worth of silver is used in making the breastplate; so that every chief represented as he stood, at least one hundred and fifty dollars,—a rich prize to the enemy who took him. I thought of this as I saw them with the first faint light of the morning sunshine glancing off and on their silver decorations as they moved busily about, giving orders in quite sharp, decided tones, which told us that they knew what they were doing, and expected to be obeyed. Each of them wore a cap of many colors, blue, red, purple, brown; and on the shoulders of some of the higher chiefs floated an elegant cape, to correspond. In front of the cap, fitted on very nicely, was a silver plate, which came over the forehead and defended the face. A tiny silver chain was fastened on the sides of the cap, and fastened under the chin, thus holding it in place. Then on top of their caps was a fine silver tassel.

They all wore sandals upon their feet, to protect them from the sharp stones during the long march which lay before them.

Each of the common soldiers, of which I was one, had a knife, a good spear, and a shield of hard, polished wood. Our "defense" consisted of a little god which had been placed in the horn of an antelope; one of these we all wore hung about our necks. These lesser gods cost from fifty cents to two dollars. They are constantly renewed; a new one being necessary every time the native man goes to battle or on a hunting expedition.

We wore pantaloons similar in cut to those worn by the Chinese, made of cotton cloth of bright colors, red and purple being the favorite and predominating hues. Our shield, fastened onto our arms, was of iron.

You can well imagine how brilliant a scene we made as we stood silently in line, waiting for marching orders.

How my heart thrilled as at length was heard, shrill and piercing, stirring the echoes for many rods around, the blast of a bugle, and we were given the signal to march! At last, oh, at last, the long looked for, long expected time had come! I was actually going to fight. No sham fight; no mock boy prisoners to be taken from behind toy forts; but a real, genuine battle lay before me, in which men would fight to the death for the honor and victory of their tribe.

It seemed as if I was treading upon air. I seemed wholly

spirited. The drums rolled out in a deafening manner, the bugles and horns cut the air with their sharpness, and the hoarse cheers, and cries, and songs of the native men and women, and of the children who flocked about us, called me back to earth and realities.

Father walked in front, resplendent in a long cloak made of every color imaginable, skillfully embroidered in silver and gold. I kept my eyes fixed upon him, and my heart swelled at the thought that perhaps I should one day hold a similar position. We marched along steadily, keeping in line and being very orderly, until we had left Bendoo far behind us.

There were fifteen hundred of us boys, not any of us being over eighteen years of age ; and after a halt had been called, and we were gathered about a camp fire that night, we lost all restraint, and enjoyed ourselves to the fullest extent. Some of us had killed some small game, and we cooked this, and eating it, sang and told stories until it was time to cuddle up closely to one another and go to rest.

The next morning we resumed the march, crossing the Marfa in canoes. These canoes were manned by possibly fifty or sixty men. After crossing the Marfa, we marched directly southeast, until we came to the flourishing town, Tarldobah, as strongly fortified as was Bendoo. For two or three days we marched through a most beautiful country, passing large orange and banana groves, long, rolling meadows, and breaking our way through dense, majestic forests, or climbing over a fine, steep mountain.

We were marching now much as we pleased, and beguiled away the time by singing and story-telling ; but directly as we began to near the enemy's borders, the chiefs called us to order, and the rapidity with which we all fell into position was surprising. A little before noon of the fifth day we arrived, and halted, at a broad eminence overlooking the town of the enemy. It was the capital town of the Cobbars.

I noticed a look of anxiety pass over the face of some of the men who stood near me, and I overheard one of them say, "I hope it won't be me."

"What does he mean?" I asked of the kind chief who was my commander.

"He means he hopes that it will not be him who will be called upon to lose his hand," replied the chief.

Then seeing the look of inquiry upon my face, hastened to explain. "We send to the enemy a war challenge in form of a human hand. One of these men here will be called upon to sacrifice his hand. It may be you, it may be me; I do not know. It will be whoever the king may think fit to select."

Strange as it may seem, the man whom I had heard express a wish that he might not be chosen, *was* selected as the one to give his hand, and was brought before father. He dared not demur, for then, by so doing, he would have lost his life.

"Hold out your hand," father commanded. Pressing his lips together firmly, the man obeyed, and one of the soldiers came up and with his sword severed it from the wrist. A tremble passed through the man's form, but beyond that he exhibited no further sign that he was in pain and suffered. His arm was rubbed with a common ointment, which prevented him from bleeding to death, and bound up in many cotton bands. The poor fellow must have suffered, but I never heard him make a sound that showed that he was in any pain.

One of our men was selected to take this hand to the enemy. He did not return, but the hand was sent back with words of defiance by one of their men. He was instantly killed by the medicine man who accompanied us. Our man had probably suffered the same fate at the hands of the enemy.

Our army then swept down upon the town and attempted to take it by force, but were bravely repulsed. We gave them the idea that we thought ourselves defeated, and late that night, when we thought they were off guard, attacked them again, and were again driven back.

Was it possible, I asked myself, that we were going to be defeated, after having come so far, and after having felt so confident in our success? Our military strength was great, but might not that of the enemy be still greater? Our armies were well disciplined, for we had been trained from our youth in war principles and tactics; but might not this be true and truer of the besieged people?

I felt that sooner than lose this battle I would suffer any torture, endure any pain, and, if it were possible, sacrifice my life ten times over.

My father's army, I had been proud to learn, was one that was much respected and feared by the tribes for many miles around. He had not only been able to repulse all the would-be encroachers on his territory, but had conquered and subdued many powerful peoples who had occupied land he wished to possess.

Oh, the gods wouldn't let my first battle end in defeat! At daybreak the next morning we fell upon their fortifications for the third time. Our commanding officer Mormoro Jiffy, in African urged us on with fiery eloquence to fight, and eager for victory we needed but little urging. A great amount of bloodshed and death took place on both sides : the men were excited, for between these two tribes was a grudge of long standing.

At the end of ten hours we succeeded in destroying the fortifications and entered their town. They were gathered in line to meet us, so near the walls that we were actually in spear throw of one another, and we did most of our fighting on both sides with the spear. It is the distinguishing weapon of the Vey man. The ones we used were from five to six feet in length, and were made of oak, with the diagonal end of the best steel, finely sharpened and tempered. We fought a hand-to-hand fight, and many lost their lives.

For myself I seemed to bear a charmed life. My spear was broken, and Mormoro Jiffy thrust a gun and shot into my hand. It was the second time in my life that I had ever handled a gun, and finding this one placed in my hands so suddenly, somewhat confused and embarrassed me. In the excitement of the moment I thrust all the caps and shot into the muzzle of the gun and rammed them forcibly down. When I fired it off it recoiled with much force, and the backward action was so powerful that it took away my breath for an instant, and made me, as you say in this country, "see stars."

Fortunately I was not stunned, and could resume the fight, taking care to procure another spear. I was sure of this. I knew it would serve me no mean trick. We fought hand-to-hand for eight long hours, then we managed to set their town on fire ; and then by a skillful manœuvre, which is commonly practiced by the native tribes, we forced the enemy backward into the flames.

They had lost many men and we far outnumbered them, and seeing no hope of victory they surrendered and became our prisoners. Their town was now our town, and their provisions our provisions.

How happy was I when I heard the welcome cry, "We surrender, we surrender." I was considerably wounded, and my clothes hung upon my back in tatters, but I didn't care for anything. We had won! We were victorious! The gods had been propitious, and I was very grateful to them.

The next morning, as was the custom, the captives who were rebellious and haughty were beheaded, many of them dying in the spirit of heroes.

I wanted to be a warrior now more than ever. Much elated, we returned to Bendoo, driving our prisoners before us like sheep. Maybe a few words more on the war customs of my people gleaned from the experience of later years would be of interest.

Over the army the king is commander-in-chief, who seldom, if ever, fights himself, but who reviews troops before and after battle, and promotes or condemns to death, as it suits his whim. He is always pleased to commend valor, as he is quick to punish cowardice. Nothing is despised quite so much by the Vey man as lack of courage. If a soldier is detected in shirking any duty while on the battlefield, he is instantly killed by his chief, while his memory and name, and the names of all connected with him, are held in the greatest contempt and scorn.

When a king is about to begin a battle, he places his men much in the following manner. The younger men, who are desirous of winning honors, are placed in the front ranks, at once the place of distinction and danger.

They are placed in this way to protect the older and more skilled warriors behind them, from the first hot charge of the enemy. These "boys" fight usually with a vim and earnestness which some who are older than they might do well to imitate. I know how it was in my own case.

I knew that some of the men behind me were narrowly watching all my movements, to see if I was skillful in the use of my weapon, and brave or not. I knew, also, that if I was inclined to retreat from the danger before me, there was as certain a danger behind, for some old warrior would take my life before I had retreated a dozen steps.

There is nothing left, then, to the boys but fight, and fight they do ; often covering themselves with glory in the eyes of the army by their tact, and persistency, and skill.

This courage seems to be innate with them ; and, as I have said before, a good deal depends upon the excellent discipline which they receive ; and also upon the spirit of emulation caused by the presence of the older men, who they know will report to the king all their deeds.

After a battle, the first thing an army does is what we did after the capture of Tarldobah ; *i. e.,* take possession of all the cattle they can find, all the sheep and goats, and all the grain and maize they can lay their hands on, and appropriate to themselves anything to which they may take a fancy.

Tarldobah as we marched away, after sacking it, presented a bare and wretched appearance enough.

CHAPTER IX.

AT THE MISSION.

" In man's most dark extremity,
    Oft succor dawns from heaven."
                                —*Byron.*

" I knew not all—yet
    Something of unrest
    Set on my heart."
                            —*Hemans.*

AFTER THE WAR—DAYS IN BENDOO.

SHORTLY after our return to Bendoo, father appointed a day to receive the chiefs and the men who had fought under them. Never shall I forget that day — beautiful beyond description, not a cloud to be seen !

The soldiers were grouped together, wondering among themselves who were to be promoted and who would lose their lives ; hinting darkly that this one's head would not be on his shoulders at sunset, or giving their opinion that such a one would be made chief, at least.

I was very anxious indeed concerning my fate. My heart thumped as the hour of the interview drew near. At last we heard echoing throughout the town the rumbling roll of the kettle-drum, which announced to us that father was in waiting to review us.

He was seated in state in the courtyard before his palace, with his councilors grouped about him. Very handsome and splendid he looked, in a beautiful scarlet jacket and a white undershirt, both of which were finely embroidered with gold and silver filigree work. The chiefs took their places on either side of him, in order of their rank, while a little to the right of him were his drummers, dancers, and musicians.

One by one the chiefs came up to him, and, prostrating themselves before him, named over the brave men and then the unfortunate ones who had exhibited cowardice. The former were given an advance in rank, while the slaughter of the latter men was something awful. The councilors tried in vain to change father's decision where some of the men were concerned, but he was inexorable. In Bendoo, at the present time, this wholesale butchery after a battle is not indulged in as it was then. The councilors seem to have become possessed of more power to prevent such scenes, and certainly have more influence with their kings than they had with my father, who was a self-willed, determined man, who used his despotic power to its fullest extent.

A few of the strongest men suspected of cowardice were granted their lives; but for my own part, I would have preferred death to the contempt and scorn with which they were treated by their companions. Jeered and sneered at, and tabooed from all pleasure and companionship, they were left alone. Cowardice is something we never forget, never forgive.

Then, as I have described before, the prisoners whom we captured were brought up before father. Each one was asked: " Are you willing to become a faithful subject to me? Are you willing to fight, to die for me?"

I pray I may never see so much blood shed again as I did that day. The courtyard and streets were red with it, and it trickled off the stones of the street in the vicinity like water. For my own part, I was glad when it was over and father had dismissed those who were left; but I judge that the others enjoyed it, and were sorry when the last poor wretch moaned out his death cry. That evening we had, as is the custom after battle, a war dance.

For a time everything was quiet in my life, and secretly I chafed at this quiet, like a young race horse that has tasted the joys of the track, and is eager to be upon it again, winning fresh honors and plaudits. I was thrilled with the remembrance of my first battle, and was eager and anxious for an active life. I looked upon the games in which the boys indulged, with secret contempt. What child's play they seemed after the reality of war. Most of the time was spent in hunting, and in making eyes at the girls who were beginning to return from their isolated schools in great numbers, and were ready to become the wife of any one who could pay the sum asked for them.

I ought to speak briefly concerning the women of Vey,— their character and condition,—and perhaps as well here as elsewhere. They are for the most part good, decent, and, comparatively speaking, very well-behaved. They are very great smokers, and consume as much tobacco as a man. Some of them, too, are great drinkers, but, I am glad to say, these are exceptional cases.

A Vey mother is very kind to her children, as in the case of my own mother; they are sometimes even gentle and tender.

As the girls of my own town grew from childhood to girlhood, I noticed that they were not treated with the consideration and respect that is shown to the males. However, they were seldom abused, as are the women of some tribes. Indeed, in most parts of barbarous Africa women are treated but a little better than the lower animals.

I am glad to say, that if not shown the *greatest* respect among Vey and Mandingo, they are, at least, shown some; and a few of my father's favorite wives, especially Taradobah, had a great deal to do with managing his affairs.

I think the women are happy and contented. They were not at that time, and are not now, like many African women, slaves, but understood how to make the most of their charms to coax and wheedle about their husbands, and, as I used to see, with much amusement, get the upper hand of them. After all, human nature is the same the wide world over, and women are the cleverest diplomats under the sun, for their modes and ways of obtaining their desired ends are such that a man does not understand, and therefore cannot cope with.

I remember one chief, Hallo by name, had a vixenish wife of whom he was very tired. He decided to cast her off, and sent her back to her parents. What happened? Like a swarm of angry bees buzzing about his ears, and threatening to sting him to death, the whole female population of Bendoo surrounded his hut. They abused him in no gentle terms, commanded him to take back his wife, and to treat her kindly forever afterwards, and declared they would stand about his home, and keep him penned up till he starved to death, if he did not obey them.

Awed by their number and their shrill chattering and screaming, he was glad to be rid of them, chose the lesser of two evils, and took back his wife. They made him promise that he would never again turn her from him.

Poor Hallo! I was extremely sorry for him, and made up

my mind to never, never marry, as I watched that scolding
crowd of women disperse to their various homes.   The women
do not love each other in particular, but they do protect one
another from any fancied wrong, and all resent a fancied slight
or grievance put upon one of their number.

At the school to which they are sent they are taught many
useful trades, and they make their living by working at these
trades ; and some of the women do very fine work indeed.
They embroider with gold and silver thread the tunics and
togas of the king and chiefs ; and some of it was truly exquisite.
I have often stood and watched a native girl at work embroidering, and the quietness and ease with which she worked silver
palm trees, golden elephants, moons, half-moons, and running
vines, was really wonderful.   Then others are hairdressers, and
do nothing else but go around among the richer natives, comb-
ing, oiling, and arranging their hair for them, on an average of
three times every week.   Inscriptions to the gods are cut upon
the silver shields and defenses worn at war time by the chiefs,
and it is the women who sometimes cut them.   Besides these
there are housekeepers, singers, dancers, and sewers.   Each
woman is taught something useful.   And this fact of having
ability in some line cannot but help in uplifting the women,
and teaching them self-respect, as nothing else can.

They do not break the ground to any extent ; and the
wives of poor men grind the corn for their bread between large,
flat stones ; and when a place has been cleared of wood, and
the brush burnt by the men, the rest of the soil cultivation is
left for the poorer class of women.

Father's wives were never obliged to perform manual labor.
The wives of kings seldom, if ever, are obliged to do so.

My mother and Taradobah were especially favored by father ;
mother because of her high birth, Taradobah because of her
position as best-loved wife.   They had little if anything to do,
and his other wives waited on them, obeyed their slightest wish,
as if they had been slaves, which in one respect they were.
When father would take a new wife, Taradobah used to seem
pleased, and say to mother, "One more servant to run for us."

Since each chief had so many wives, things did not always
go so pleasantly and harmoniously as he could have wished
them.   I distinctly remember some of the domestic broils
which often took place, and strengthened my vow to lead a life

of celibacy. Naturally enough, there was a good deal of jealousy among the wives as to the one who should be first in their husband's affections.

In most cases they managed to hide their feelings bravely enough, and made no demur when hurt or angry. Once or twice, to the best of my recollection, the women got into serious quarrels among themselves. They were very serious indeed, for they came to bloodshed, and before their anger had spent itself and become appeased, several of their number were wounded. In this way they vented upon each other the angry feelings they dared not show before their lords and masters.

There were two women of one chief who were furiously jealous of each other; one day they disagreed. Their example became contagious, and spread rapidly around among the others who were near enough to know of it. They flocked to the scene of the combat, and dog-like entered into it, striking out right and left, and biting with a vim and enthusiasm worthy of a better cause. In this instance the men were called upon to separate them; which they accomplished after some time with the aid of stout wooden clubs.

The young girls who came from school had, many of them, rather beautiful forms, which I much admired. They were full and rounded, without being grossly fat, and, what is better still, they keep their beauty of contour quite late in life; which is something peculiar to them, I think, most African women becoming hideously emaciated as the years go on, or just as hideously gross and fleshy.

Their limbs have not been subjected to the restraints of an absurd amount of clothing; and their waists are not compressed, like the waists of the civilized woman.

I have seen many of my native women who were as finely formed as are any of the representations of an ideal Venus in art.

The Vey girl does not wear clothing of any kind until she reaches the age of ten. Then she puts on an apron made of the skin of some animal. As she grows older, she wears a cloak or tunic wrapped about her, and fastened on one shoulder. If she be the favorite wife of a wealthy man, then this mantle is plentifully and elaborately trimmed and decorated with beads and silver work. She wears gaudy bracelets and anklets, and gold and silver hair ornaments. She goes forth "the mold of fashion, the glass of form—the observed of all observers," filling the less fortunate of her sex with ill-concealed envy at the sight.

The poorer women have no gold or silver, and make up for this deficiency by wearing brass and tin jewelry; and fastening up their hair with thorns, aiming to look as fine and attractive as they can.

Of the king's wives, she who can boast of the highest birth holds the keys of what is known as the "storehouse." The storehouse is a large hut, in which is kept the food and clothing of the king's wives. I have spoken of this in connection with my own mother, who held this position.

I have spoken at length, also, of the Amazons,—the position they hold, their character, and the duties which they owe to society.

There are the women known as "the dancers." They do nothing else but dance, and are as graceful and fleet of foot as so many Atalantas.

How much my people loved dancing, and how much they danced! I was very fond of it myself, and used to enter into it with more zest at this time than I put into anything else, except, possibly, fighting; for I was too eager and anxious for another battle to be content with the rather monotonous life which Bendoo presented at this time.

We began to dance at sundown, and continued it till long after midnight.

"When the sun goes down all Africa dances," is a common phrase, and a true one.

We might almost be called "the dancing tribe," we are so fond of it.

The girls go through the steps of the various dances with a peculiar undulation and grace of body, and enter into it with so much zest and evident enjoyment, that the latter emotion always proves contagious to the onlooker. The forms of the girls are adapted to artistic posing; and though they are all unconscious of it, they often make very fine pictures and groups, seeming to have an innate sense of the artistic. It is difficult for me to say which are the better dancers, the young girls or the boys.

We—a dozen or more of us—girls and boys would dance ourselves into a wild frenzy,—dance till we had completely lost the control of our limbs, which whirled and dashed us about, twisted and turned our bodies in a fashion that takes away the breath. The on-lookers enjoyed the "frenzy" dance exceedingly, while the musicians kept time with these violent movements as best they could. Sometimes we danced alone, or singly ; and sometimes we danced in groups, singing or chanting in a wild, weird way,—especially true in times of honor festivals given to the gods, or at wedding or funeral services.

Altogether it used to be a pretty, interesting scene in the cool, delicious moonlight evenings,—the red light of the fires that were burning incense to some god, shedding their light over the dancing figures, and the dark faces and picturesque costumes of the spectators.

One of the women—she who was considered the best dancer—was constituted a kind of leader, and she flung her limbs about in the wildest possible manner ; while the rest of us imitated her movements to the best of our ability.

There is nothing immodest about the dance nor the dancers, nothing that could offend the purest-minded person ; the dancers themselves were and are perfectly innocent of anything indecorous. They dance and caper about with as little thought of impropriety as a child would have or a kitten.

At our evening enjoyments there was always a great deal of noise, for noise was one of the chief elements of a good time. These were some of the happiest moments in my life, if I had only known of it.

After we were wearied with dancing we gathered about the fires, and laughed and joked at one another's expense ; and sang in such a wild, witchy way, that I doubt if you would have called it singing. This singing was always accompanied with the drum, and the songs we sang were usually the compositions of one of the medicine-men.

Every month we had what was known by the people as the "giant dance." Father would appoint one of the lesser priests to carefully watch the people of Bendoo for one month, to spy out their faults and failings, and make note of them. It was the duty of this priest to find out who of the people were liars, who deceivers or thieves, who were scandalmongers, and who were scolds, and to discover those men who were abusive to their wives and children. All the lazy ones and idle ones were watched, and their names taken note of, as were also the names of those who were lax in performing the duties and respects which they owed to the king and the gods.

The people know that they are being watched, but it is seldom they are able to discover the spy.

As the first silver rim of a new moon begins to glimmer in the sky, the "giant dance" takes place. The priest, elevated on a pair of high stilts, with flowing robes of brilliant hues covering these, and resembling the famous giantess of storybooks, stalks majestically through the town, armed with a big, stout stick.

He was at liberty to enter the huts of any who had proved themselves worthy of punishment, and beat the inmates as severely as he pleased. The degree of severity exercised in their chastisement depended, of course, upon the degree of their offense. The people had no right to defend themselves; they could do nothing but yield, and bear with the blows as best they knew how. Woe to the liar, the disrespectful, the scandalmonger at those times! The "giant" had no mercy upon them, and he was especially merciless to the liar.

After he had gone the rounds, and chastised those who had deserved it, he executed a queer, impromptu dance, and presented a comical and ludicrous sight enough, hopping about like a distressed mountain, on his stiff, wooden legs.

It used to surprise me a good deal at the number of huts found vacant, whose owners found pressing business out of town when it was time for the "giant dance"—a case, I presume, where guilty consciences need no accusers; and so the men and women were prone to flee from the medicine-man's rod of correction.

I was punished once or twice myself, on the strength of a fancied or real disrespect shown to one of the old chiefs.

It was only natural that I should become enamored of some of the girls. I became very fond of a tall, well-formed girl, the daughter of a chief, Zuse by name.

Until I expressed my admiration for Zuse in little warmer terms than usual, we had been together in the games and dances; but as soon as I hinted to father that I cared for her, and would like to make her my wife, we were separated, and allowed to have no communication with each other. At that time Zuse and I were both very young, but marriages contracted at an early age were not at all rare, but extremely common. Father did not favor my suit at all. He told me that he desired that I should wait, and if I wanted the girl for my wife, he would see that she was kept for me till I was older. I thought this was very hard, and eyed Zuse from a distance with melancholy eyes. I was much given to attending marriage ceremonies, and trying to imagine myself in the bridegroom's place with Zuse as the bride. Poor Zuse, I wonder where she is to-day! How many changes have taken place since then!

I have explained how negotiations are entered into between the parents of the young people wishing to marry. If the consent of both is gained, then, like Zuse and myself, the young couple are sedulously kept apart until the day of their marriage.

The bride is led to the priests by her mother. They are attended by a sister of the bridegroom elect, if he chance to have one; if not, then some other one of his female relatives takes this place, which is considered one of much honor, only second to that of the medicine-man. This relative is one who has always afterwards much to say and do in the future home of the contracting parties.

The marriage ceremony was a strange mingling of the native and outside customs. An article of clothing is given in place of the customary ring known in this country. After marriage the girls remain with their parents till their husbands have built them huts. When this is completed she left the home of her people, and, accompanied by the women of the district, went to her husband's hut. The women who went with her grouped about the door and chanted doleful and dreary melodies, supposed to express their sorrow for the loss of their friend.

They twisted their bodies about like the contortionists that they were, and called down the blessings of all the gods upon their heads. Then, still chanting their gloomy songs, withdrew from the hut and left the bride to her husband and to peace.

The skin of a Vey babe at its birth is very white, and months pass sometimes before it assumes the hue of its parents.

When a child is born the medicine-man is called. He anoints it with ointments, rubbing these into small incisions which he makes upon the child's body.

The baby is strapped on the back of its mother, who thus carries it about everywhere with her, till it grows to be quite a large child. It is kept in place on her back by means of a wide strip of soft skin, that is sometimes lined with soft cotton. This is passed about her waist in a manner that leaves a kind of pouch behind, and in this the babe lies snugly and safely. It is often made of an antelope skin, and when belonging to a rich chief's wife, was finely embroidered. In such a cradle as I have described I spent my infant days.

One day, as I played in a half-hearted fashion with the boys,—for my whole mind was in the future battles that might take place,—I heard that Zolusingbe had come from the school, and was dying in the hut of a medicine-man. With real sorrow I went to him. He had been bitten by a cobra. He was so swollen and disfigured with pain, that I had some difficulty in recognizing my old friend. He smiled feebly when I entered the hut, and held out his hand to me.

"I am going, Besolow," he said ; "ask the gods to allow me to go to Igenie. Be a brave warrior always. Never run ; die a thousand times over before you will be a coward." He died that night, and was sincerely mourned, for he was an old, well-beloved chief.

His body was treated with the utmost respect, and, as is the custom, was buried a few hours after death ; in this case the funeral services took place before sunrise the next day.

We had a cemetery portioned off in each district for the burial of the dead, and to the one at the outskirts of Bendoo, he was reverently borne in the arms of two of the priests.

Musicians with drums and clappers played airs as doleful and woeful as you can imagine. I remember those who had no drums came with tin pans and sharply polished sticks. An appropriate song was sung.

High ideas of music have never been cultivated by my people ; but such ideas as they do possess, they enjoy and employ to their utmost.

The war weapons of Zolusingbe were laid about his grave with his favorite food ; and a half-dozen cattle were killed. This is true in the case of all funeral ceremonies. All the worldly possessions of the deceased man or woman are placed around their grave. A Vey cemetery presents a somewhat odd and grotesque appearance.

Before Zolusingbe's hut a sacred fire was kept burning for many days, and attended to with the utmost love and care. This to light and warm the spirit if it be floating in space, and not as yet consigned to Igenie.

I mourned a great deal for my old friend ; but soon I had a terrible fancied trouble of my own, that for the time quite drove all thoughts of anybody else from my mind. My father was again talking of sending me to Cape Mount Mission. In vain mother pleaded with him not to send me away; in vain, also, was all Taradobah's reasoning ; in vain all my mother's sacrifices to the gods : father remained obdurate, and declared that go I should.

I wept, and besought him not to send me among those horrible people with the white skin and hair. I took no consolation from his words that they were not "horrible," but were very kind, and would treat me well.

Every morning I feared lest he should bind me, and unknown to my mother and Taradobah, bear me off willy nilly.

Bitterly my mother grieved. Dear mother ! She loved me very dearly, and she felt sure that if I went away she would never see me again.

CHAPTER X.

"It is no small conquest to overcome yourself."—*Old Proverb.*

"Harken, harken!
God speaketh in thy soul:
I am the end of love;
Give love to me."
— *Mrs. Browning.*

AT THE MISSION.

FOR a time it seemed that mother and Taradobah would prevail upon father not to send me away, for he ceased talking about it, and left me in peace. "My dear boy, my dear Besolow," my mother would say to me, "I would rather have you die before my eyes than have you sent away, I know not where."

"My mother," I would reply, "I would much sooner die than go; pray that my father may not send me." My father's chief interpreter, if I may so term him, was a bright young negro, who had come from the southern part of the United States of America, and who had more advanced ideas on most matters pertaining to civilization than anyone in our territory. Father thought a great deal of Curtis, and Curtis seemed to have father's interests very much at heart.

Father did an extensive trade in liquor and tobacco. The traders who brought these commodities to our territory were dealers in Boston, Massachusetts, Holland, Belgium, Portugal, Spain, England, and especially in Germany. Germany sent more liquor to our shores than all the other countries. It is and was a miserable shame, and a disgrace to the men who burlesque the name of civilization, to bring their poor rum and poisonous tobacco, and put it in the way of ignorant, hot-headed, excitable savages, who under its influence grew more degraded and less responsible for their actions. It is the strongest subject of which I can think for a temperance lesson. In many cases all good that might be accomplished by the missionaries is set at naught by the evil of drink. Is there nothing that can and may be done to prevent this contemptible traffic between rum-dealers and ignorant savages? They come to our shores with their devilish wares, and take away in exchange immense quantities of gold dust, valuable ivory, and other rich products of our land too numerous to mention.

Such an unfair, one-sided, contemptible business ought to be stopped. Right here I would like to speak of another disgrace; this time it falls upon the English people. In exchange for our wares, the same ship that may bring to our shores a missionary, brings thousands of *carved and decorated idols for us to worship!*

Think of it! Give it but a moment's consideration! What must be the minds, what must be the nature, of the men who have these idols made to sell to the unfortunate, credulous African! These facts are food for thought; and they should be pondered by all who are interested in banishing heathenism from the "Dark Continent."

The young Southerner, Curtis, saw what evil results were following in the train of the immense rum traffic, and, as I afterwards learned, tried in every way to have my father cease trading in it; but father was obdurate, and closed his eyes to the misery it was causing. He had immense warehouses on the coast. To these barrels and barrels of cheap, villainous whiskey and poor rum were sent up the Niger River and Peso, on the banks of which were other stations of his. The liquor would go from one to the other; and as it passed from place to place it would be drank freely, and the whole population of a town would often be beastly intoxicated at one time.

I remember, in Bendoo, when I was quite a youth, my father had on hand hundreds and thousands of gallons of whiskey, gin, and wine of all kinds. When Bendoo was seem·ingly in her best condition, and everything looked prosperous, and my father was accumulating vast wealth from this traffic, a king of Lake Tchad region, of the Cossa tribe, Cobbar by name, besieged Bendoo for three days and three nights. The town becoming pressed for lack of food and water, father was defeated, and the Cossas took Bendoo into their possession. They began to drink much of the liquors, till they became intoxicated, and like mad men they fell upon the helpless inhabitants of the town. They butchered their captives in the

most cruel manner; completely sacked Bendoo; gathered
together all the relatives of the king, and killed and tortured
them to death, one by one. They took some of the captives,
those who had escaped the knife or fire, outside of the barricade
which they had raised. I was one of these captives. Cobbar
came to me in person, and asked me my preference, whether I
should rather go with him to his territory as a captive, and with
the thought that my father, who had escaped from the maraud-
ers, might rescue me, or should I prefer to be butchered. I
I was not afraid, and so I looked him directly in the eye, and
said calmly, "I have no choice, King Cobbar; I leave the
matter entirely with you."

Mother was with me, and when she saw how disconcerned
I was about saving my life, she whispered to me to be respect-
ful and humble, and accept the former proposition of my
captor. She said she would see to it that father redeemed me
very soon. I listened to mother, and told Cobbar that I would
return with him, though I never expected to return alive.
Then he told my mother that she might take her departure,
as it is a custom among the Cossa people to release all female
captives when they shall have taken a town and sacked it;
but my mother refused to leave me. She told Cobbar that
she should rather he would kill her than force her to go without her son.

Cobbar at this time was greatly disappointed, for when he
besieged Bendoo he made sure that he had blockaded and surrounded the town so securely that my father would easily
fall into his possession; but by the aid of imperial guards
father cut his way through the whole lines of Cobbar and
escaped. It was one of the most daring exploits that Bendoo
men, who are nothing, if not daring, forced their way through
the whole Cossa army; bravely dying or falling wounded on
every side, but caring for nothing so long as they were enabled
to bear my father and their well-beloved king to a place of
safety; and in this noble and loyal attempt they were successful.

It is a wonder at this point that Cobbar, who was much
enraged and chagrined at father's escape, should have saved the
lives of any of his relatives; but the spirit moved him, and he
took mother and myself in his train, and leaving Bendoo he
went into Tocoroh, one of father's fortified cities that had been
sacked by Cobbar two weeks before he had besieged Bendoo.

He made this town his headquarters. It was built on four hills, bearing similarity to old Rome. On the left-hand side, towards the region of Abyssinia, ran the River Peso. Over this is built a bridge about one fourth of a parasang. The river itself is about ten plethron. After Cobbar had entered the stronghold he prepared to receive an attack, which he expected might come from the western part of the town, for that was the most vulnerable point to attack. By this very fact he was misled. Father had many hundred native soldiers, stole a march upon him, by making a nocturnal attack on the *eastern* side. He had the bridge cut down and had climbed the barricades with his soldiery, and was besieging the town almost before Cobbar and his men knew it. They were taken completely off their guard.

When he had to some degree recovered his equilibrium, Cobbar turned all his forces of arms towards father and the eastern part of the town. Then about one half of father's men stole around and attacked him from the rear. Then arose the clamor of war, the twang of bow and arrow, the whizzing sound of spear. The conflict continued for many hours, till Cobbar, hard pressed on all sides, began to yield.

While all this was going on your humble servant, bound hands and feet among the other captives, was wondering how long the battle would last, and whispering petitions to the gods that my father might be victor. With bated breath we, myself and captives, talked over the probable result of the battle. Mother, as most women would have done, began to cry, and was very despondent. She heard a man say in Vey that the battle was lost to our people. From the eminence upon which she stood, through the mist, she thought she could see some of the forces of father, and they were retreating. She clasped her hands and moaned pitifully. I restrained her from giving vent to her fret and worry all that I could, but it availed me nothing. In the midst of her moaning a very dear young fellow, Mumbru, who lay close beside me, was shot by an arrow in the left side by some of the soldiers below the hill, and he died in a few minutes. In almost the same breath another man received an arrow in the eye. The wound bled profusely, and in a short time he bled to death, internally. Mother stopped her moaning then, to attend to the needs of the dying, suffering men.

After a hard fight Cobbar was defeated, and father became master of the town once more. He relieved mother and me, and the rest of the prisoners; and then Cobbar—who was not fortunate enough to escape as father had done—and his soldiery were made prisoners of war.

The next morning, at about eight o'clock, 250 men in civilized armor came from the Republic of Liberia to assist and give aid to my father if he had been in want of it. He thanked them heartily, but told them, what they could easily see for themselves, that they were just too late. The battle was over; the struggle was ended.

At ten o'clock Cobbar and the men imprisoned with him were brought into the market-place. Father asked Cobbar what he should do with him.

Cobbar told him that he could do whatever he felt disposed under the circumstances. Father questioned him as to his purpose of entering his territory. He asked Cobbar if he had been instigated by some other party or parties, or if some relative of his (father's) had persuaded him to besiege Bendoo. He said a friend of father's, one Barlakikbaila, had persuaded him to do what he had.

A messenger was despatched to Baila. The messenger soon returned. Baila emphatically denied that he had done anything towards persuading Cobbar towards making an invasion of Vey territory. The next day Baila came himself with 1,500 or 1,600 men, all heavily armed.

A court-martial was held, and to this court-martial all the chiefs in the vicinity were summoned; and especially those whom Cobbar had implicated in anyway concerning the attack on Bendoo. Each and every one of these affirmed that they had not had anything to do with the affair.

Then said father to Cobbar, "What hast thou to say for thyself? Thine own words have made thee a liar." According to our court-martial laws, especially among the Mandingo and Vey, a man having been found guilty of such a traitorous act is put to death by the sword of the king, especially if the convict be a king. So Cobbar was bound hands and feet with the men who were captured with him and taken to a place of safe-keeping.

Here he was beheaded by father's own hand, and the other captives were put to death by the other men.

These disagreeable duties over, the court-martial disbanded, and we returned to Bendoo. The dear town of my birth was buried in ashes. Such a great sadness filled my heart at the sight. For the first and last time in my life I saw my father lean on his spear and weep, as his eye took in the sad state of affairs in his once flourishing town. I do not think he wept so much over the loss of money and property, as he did over his defeat in the first contest with Cobbar. That was a circumstance which he felt to be more or less of a disgrace; and the property which he lost was no slight loss. A great many people have erroneous ideas on this point. They think when we speak of African chiefs and kings that they haven't anything. Now, they are very much mistaken; they are laboring under false impressions.

My own father, King Carttom, was a very wealthy man. I can bring Messrs. Wilber & Broom, Chiswick & Bros., the former in Hamburg the latter in England, also Werner & Co., Hamburg, as witnesses that father lost over $200,000 worth of whiskey at that time. It had been spilled into the streets, drank, and burnt by Cobbar's troops. All of which now, in spite of the money loss, I think is a good thing.

I remember this very well because these various parties were father's creditors, and they pushed him very strictly for the pay, and on this account father found himself in a position that was anything but pleasant; but my father, Armah, was a vigorous man, and not easily discouraged, and so he soon paid up his debts. After he got his debts paid he rebuilt Bendoo.

To resume the thread of my story. Curtis thought that the future welfare of the Vey land depended upon father's sons, and consequently favored the idea of having us sent to the mission, learning the English tongue, and the customs. He came to me and talked to me earnestly, and as I had never been talked to before in all my life. I liked Curtis, and so I listened to what he told me, and pondered over it afterwards.

I was fond of rum myself, and often got drunk at that young age, and so resented all that he said about what a good and glorious thing it would be for the people if it were abolished altogether, or, at least, the trade in it diminished. He persisted, and talked so well that I found myself becoming interested, and almost believing that it would be best for my people if they did not have so much liquor to drink; and promising him that if ever I had the power to restrain it, I would do so. But when he touched on the subject of my going to the mission, I flared into a temper, and declared if he said another word about it I would leave him immediately.

"Now, Besolow," he said, "listen and have patience." His African, which he had mastered in a wonderfully short time, was very stilted and stiff, but I well understood him.

"Listen to me, my boy. Why are you so averse to going away to the mission?"

"I do not want to leave my home," I said; "I do not want to leave my mother; I do not want to leave my people. I want to be a brave warrior, and take part in all the battles that may occur between my tribe and any other. I want to be a strong and powerful hunter. I want to lead the free, happy life of my people, and not go among a new, strange kind of people, who will do with me and to me as they please."

"You will only be away from your home and people a very short space of time; and when you come back, Besolow, things will appear to you in a very different light from what they do at the present."

"I do not want them to appear differently," I said stubbornly. "I am well satisfied that things should be as they are. Why should I seek a change? So long as there are plenty of battles to fight, and plenty of game to hunt, why should I desire a change? I do not."

"At the mission, my boy, you would see such superior ways of living, that you would be dissatisfied with the present state of affairs.

"All the more reason, then, that I should not go, Curtis. Zolusingbe used to teach us that contentment with our lot was something to be acquired and kept always, if we cared for happiness."

"Contentment with our lot in life is all very well, Besolow; but the people or person without an ambition, without an aim in life, don't amount to very much after all."

He saw that I could not comprehend or grasp this last meaning of his, so he began again to talk of the mission and the white people.

"There is nothing about the white people to fear, Besolow. I have lived among them all my life."

"And are alive!" I said in amazement, "and not crippled

or bewitched!" "Ah," with a shake of my head, "but you may be yet rendered miserable! Our gods may yet visit you with a direful punishment for passing your life with those white faces. You do not know how awful that punishment may be that will yet befall you."

"If it *were* a crime to live with white people," he answered, with a smile, "I was not to blame. I was born among them. I had no choice in the matter; but, Besolow, let me tell you about them. Let me tell you how kind they are, and how well they treat us blacks. They have great interest in us. They will teach you of the Lord Jesus Christ," he said, "and you will be glad to know of him." It was a new name to me, and I thought it the name of one of their earthly kings or chiefs; and I cared not to learn of him. The precious name so dear to me afterwards, so infinitely dear and full of meaning to me now, fell meaningless on my ear then, and growing exceedingly vexed at Curtis' persistency in talking to me of a subject at once so beyond and hateful to my comprehension, I left him, forbidding him to speak of it again to me.

Not only was Curtis continually talking to father about sending me off (for which at the time I began to hate him heartily), but a Dutch trader, Bromm, was interested also. He told him how much better his own sons would prove as interpreters than so many strangers. They would not be so apt to cheat and defraud him as those would who were not relatives. Between the two of them, father's mind was kept pretty full of the project of sending me away.

One day I went into mother's hut and found her in tears. She clasped me warmly to her breast, and wept over me bitterly. I knew the cause, and instinctively clung to her, and mingled my tears with her own.

"My boy, my boy, the decision is final now. You are to go away from me, and I fear I will never see you again. I dare not plead with your father any further, for he threatened me with a disgraceful punishment if I did. Oh! why is it that the gods have so disregarded my prayers? Dozens of infants have been given to the crocodiles, and prisoners innumerable have I had offered to Carnabah and the Moon. Sacred fires burn constantly before the household gods and idols, and yet, alas! alas! they have not listened—they have not heeded my supplications that my dear boy, my favorite boy, may remain with me."

"When am I going, mother?" I asked.

"I do not know. Very soon. Perhaps to-day."

"Oh!" I said bitterly; and added, with a fire that makes me ashamed to remember, "May the curses of all the gods, who did not grant our prayers,—yours and mine,—fall upon the heads of Bromm and Curtis, who have brought this thing about! May they never know a moment's peace, and upon their death, languish in Cayanpimbi forever!"

"Amen!" said my mother. "I will *not* go," I said. "Good-bye, mother." An idea had flashed upon my mind as I stood there; I would run away! I bade her an affectionate good-bye and took to the woods. How desolate and lonely I felt, fleeing farther and farther away from the people who afterwards were my best friends. How strange it seems to me now, that strange aversion and fear that filled my heart towards the white people. I believe, nay, I know, that I would willingly have died at that time sooner than have gone to the mission. For two or three days I wandered about in the thick woods, evading the searchers father had sent to find me; but at length they overtook me, and, bound hand and foot, brought me back to Bendoo and to my father. He was very angry with me. I can see his eyes flash now as they did then.

"Do you know," he said, "that I could kill you for this escapade of yours?"

"Yes," I answered fearlessly; "and I wish you would, father, rather than send me away." He approached me with short-sword uplifted as if to strike; but I calmly regarded him without moving a muscle, and as he looked into my eyes, his arm dropped to his side and he stepped back.

I was bound hand and foot to a tree, and severely thrashed by two men with long leather straps, under father's supervision. I can see my mother's pitying, wistful eyes as she passed me; but she dared not speak to me or give me food. When I was finally cut down I was very weak, and without waiting for my strength to return, father forced me to accompany him on a journey, the destination of which I knew only too well. Fainting and gasping by the way, father brought me through the forests to Cape Mount. We traveled, I think, for at least two days, and I was little more than a living skeleton when we finally arrived at our destination. And now I must tell you of my first view of the long-dreaded white man. We came through forests all the way, coming out very suddenly at the side of the superintendent's (Mr. Roberts) unpretending house. When we came around to the front of the house I saw the gentleman himself, seated on the piazza, reading. His back was turned slightly, and at first I did not see his face ; but upon hearing our footsteps he turned squarely about, and then for *the first time in my life, strange as it may seem, I looked upon the face of a white man.*

My heart beat violently as, rising, he came towards us with an outstretched hand and a smile upon his face. I didn't know what to do—whether to stand my ground or run.

As I stood deliberating upon which course of action to decide, Mrs. Roberts, his wife, came to the door. Alas ! *one* of these odd, new kind of people was bad enough ; but *two* of them were more than my valor was proof against. I told foot to help body, and ran back into the woods as rapidly as my enfeebled condition would allow. Father came after me, while Curtis explained to Mr. Roberts who I was and the purpose for which I had come, and had, I suppose, a good part, if not all of the business transactions completed before father brought me back, a trembling, wretched boy enough. Mrs. Roberts came down the piazza steps with a reassuring smile upon her lips.

I huddled to my father's side, and clenched his hand in a grasp that, with all his strength, he found it impossible to unclasp.

"Send it away !" I cried to him, "send it away !" and I screamed in fear as she approached nearer to me.

"Now, Besolow," said father, "you are acting the part of a coward, and if they had you in Bendoo, they would kill you as one. I am surprised and disappointed in you, for I thought that my son was a brave boy." This had the effect of composing me somewhat, but did not alleviate my fear in the slightest, and I begged father piteously to take me back again to Bendoo. When they attempted to lead me up the piazza steps, I flung myself face downward in the dust, which I beat in clouds about me, calling upon the gods at the top of my voice to have pity upon me, and to either kill me or save me from the threatened fate. I think father became so enraged at my conduct that he would have killed me then if it hadn't been for the interference of Mr. and Mrs. Roberts. When they found

that they could not prevail upon me to go peacefully, they were
obliged to bind me hand and foot, and in this manner they
carried me into the house and up the stairs, and left me in a
narrow little room, locking the door securely after them. I do
not like to think of that time. When I do I fall into the weak-
ness of pitying myself.

I lay helpless on the floor of the room. A stranger in a
strange place, I moaned, and sobbed, and almost died of agony ;
and at last, tired, over-taxed nature asserted itself, and with the
miserable tears clinging to my face, I fell asleep. I was awakened by somebody entering the room. It was too dark for me
to see whom, and I lay trembling and wondering what the
errand of the person could be. " Well, Besolow, are you
awake ? " It was father's voice, and I drew a relieved sigh as I
answered " Yes, sir."

" And have you made up your mind to behave yourself? "
" Yes, sir." " That is well. Now listen : these people will
treat you kindly. Learn what they have to teach as soon as
you can, and then you may return." He undid the bindings
and assisted me to rise. I could scarcely stand upon my feet,
I was so weak, and staggered from side to side like a drunken
man.

" Now good-bye," he said, and he took my hand in his.
" Good-bye." I faltered. I was determined to be brave, but
it cost me more of an effort than I can well explain, to refrain
from flinging myself at his feet and imploring to be taken back
home again. Curtis came to bid me good-bye, but I turned
my back and would have no words with him. When he persisted in talking, and trying to reconcile me to the inevitable,
I wheeled about on him with a suddenness that startled him.
" It is you who has done this," I said. "I hate you for it,
and if you do not go I will kill you ! " He left the room, not,
I think, because he was afraid of my threat, but because he saw
how useless it was to try to reason with me then.

Somebody came and placed some yams inside the door ;
but I partook of nothing till morning. I felt like a wild beast
who has had the great forest for his home, and is caught
suddenly and kept in a six by ten cage.

In the morning I heard a step outside. I shrank into the
farthest corner and buried my face in my hands. I suddenly
felt upon my arm a soft, caressing touch. It made me think

of my mother, and with a sudden calm I looked up into the face of the kind Mrs. Roberts. She was a short, plump lady, with an intelligent, kindly face and a profusion of sleek, black hair. Nothing very formidable about her.

"Besolow," she said, in a sweet voice but very bad African, "will you come downstairs with me now and have some breakfast?" I threw her hand off my arm rudely, and buried my face from sight. I am afraid she must have thought me a hopeless case, for without another word she left the room, locking it after her. As she went away and left me alone with my thoughts again, I began to cry in a hopeless, dreary way. Distinctly I remember some of the thoughts that flitted through my brain. Doubts of the gods! Could there be gods, after all? Surely if there had been they would have listened to my earnest prayers, and granted them; then a sudden fear took possession of me as I thought of how sacrilegious were my thoughts! What terrible affliction might be visited upon me for entertaining such disrespectful ideas! Humbly enough I begged their forgiveness.

What was this king Jesus Christ like, of whom the white people thought so much? He was white, like them, of course. Was he a very wonderful king? Oh, how many long days passed before it was mine to realize *what* a mighty and wonderful king he was!

As the day wore on, I rose from my position which I had kept almost without change since Mrs. Roberts left me, and went to the window. I glanced out fearfully. On the road I saw a half-dozen African boys playing marbles in the dust. Strong, straight, good-looking fellows, clad very oddly, I thought, in pantaloons and jacket. They seemed to be enjoying themselves. There certainly wasn't a great amount of trepidation in the sounds of the merry, noisy laughter that reached my lonely ears! I became interested in their antics, in spite of myself, and at last my own laughter called me to my senses and present condition. I left the window, and fell to wondering if after all they might not be kinder and pleasanter people than I had imagined them to be. Yes, maybe; but certainly the life would be a drear one if I was to be kept fastened up between four walls in this manner. Still, those boys had appeared happy enough. Thus, torn by doubts, and fears, and curiosity I passed the afternoon, and evening found me hungry enough to dispose of the yams. No one came near me that night, but the next morning Mrs. Roberts came to me again, and this time I was so mild and quiet that she led me out of the room and downstairs to the dining-room.

When I first cast my eyes on the furnishings of the room, I was filled with amazement. I wondered if the chairs, and sofa, and carpet, and curtains, and the thousand and one little adornments of a civilized home were made by human hands or by a being supreme. She sat down on a chair, but I was afraid to do so, although she motioned me to be seated. Afraid of the consequence that might follow disobedience, I obeyed her gesture and sat gingerly on the chair's edge. Finally breakfast was brought in and served.

Never shall I forget my astonishment at first beholding knives and forks, and the manner in which they were used. At last a half-dozen boys—some of them I recognized as the boys I had watched from the window—came in and took their places at the table, and Mr. Roberts took his place, and a place between him and his wife was assigned to me. I was astonished that she, a woman, was allowed to sit at the table and eat with us ; for among my people the women are not allowed to eat with the guests. Do not imagine the wives never eat with their husbands, because they do ; but they are never permitted to do so when there is a third person present.

They put the knife and fork into my hands, and bade me use them, telling me to watch them carefully to see how to do so. My efforts must have been ludicrous in the extreme, for, try hard as I would, I could not manipulate them properly.

How could a man, I thought, ever get enough to eat at such a niggardly meal as this? I thought it was the silliest thing for a man to have food scattered in a half-dozen different plates—salt here, butter there, meat on this plate and bread on that. What was the necessity of all this? It could have been done by putting all together and eating out of one bowl. Breakfast over, Mrs. Roberts, upon whom I kept my eyes constantly fixed, took me with her to a bare, white-walled room, that I learned afterwards to call schoolroom.

CHAPTER XI.

"I went to seek for Christ."—*Lowell.*

"By desiring what is perfectly good, even when we don't quite know what it is, and cannot do what we would, we are part of the Divine power against evil, widening the skirts of light, and making the struggle with darkness narrower."—*George Eliot.*

"Lead, kindly Light, amid the encircling gloom,
    Lead Thou me on;
The night is dark, and I am far from home;
    Lead Thou me on."—*J. H. Newman.*

STRUGGLE FOR LIGHT.

Mrs. Roberts began to teach me the alphabet immediately. She began with the letter A. She said it over and over, and obliged me to repeat it after her. She wrote it on a little blackboard, and guided my hand while I wrote it also. My thoughts were not on the lesson, however; they were far away, beyond the forests and hills, in my own town, with my own people; so I accomplished nothing in that first lesson. I was sent to the little room upstairs again, and locked in, and here the sad, miserable tears began once more to flow.

I wondered if I were my father's son. I half believed that I was not, and that he had sold me to these people. The boys I saw at breakfast, and again at dinner, were exceedingly well-behaved lads; but they spoke nothing but English, as did everybody else about the table; and so I felt strangely and more out of place than ever. Mrs. Roberts addressed herself to me once or twice, but I made no reply. Again I marveled at the scantiness of the meal, for it did look odd to see such small quantities of food on the table, when I had been used to sitting down to whole carcasses of animals.

In the afternoon she again tried to teach me the letter A, with no better success than before. She told me that I might go out and play with the other boys that evening, who were running races, and playing what in this country is known by the name "leap frog." I went out, and stood bashfully on the piazza ; but the boys did not take any notice of me, nor invite me to join in their games, and I was glad when I was ordered again to my room.

Thus the long days passed by. Can you imagine the sensations of a wild African boy fresh from the jungles, meeting from day to day people of foreign customs, and becoming used to the modes of civilized living, so different and so inferior, in his estimation, to those to which he has been accustomed?

In the mission school where I studied, I think there must have been at least a hundred youths of my own age, all more or less bright and apt, and coming from all parts of Western Africa.

Perhaps a word concerning the mission would not be amiss here. Mr. Roberts was a kind Christian man, who took a real interest in the many boys under his charge, and took particular pains to note the work and methods of all the teachers under him. He had a square wooden building, in which he and assistant teachers taught many classes every day ; and many other useful and practical trades. In his way he brought out all that was best in each of the young barbarians under his charge, in both a moral and material sense of the word.

In the mission at Monrovia, which I afterwards attended, they are taught in the same manner, and when they have mastered the trade, they are taught to earn their own living by following it.

The mission was neatly kept, and the boys seemed imbued with a sense of pride in keeping the grounds surrounding the different buildings clean and tidy, and seeing that the long, even roads that traverse the town were kept cleared of all obstacles.

I studied patiently enough trying to master the alphabet, every day, from nine o'clock in the morning till six o'clock at night, with the exception of Saturday, upon which I was allowed to hunt, and on Sunday, when we rested from all labors.

Father furnished me with the clothing required, which I found a great incumbrance ; also all the food I ate. When the messengers came with my food or other necessities demanded for me by Mrs. Roberts, I would fly to them and ask of my home and people, and of my mother. They would tell me of all the loving messages mother had sent to me, and of how sad she was since my departure, and how often she wept. This would make me weep, too ; and I would bid the messengers to tell her how unhappy I was, in my turn, and of how I longed to get away from the mission.

I was very miserable, and grew more so every day. I wished for death; anything was preferable to this mean, pent-up existence. I thought of all the bright dreams I had entertained of becoming a warrior and a brave hunter; and this life was the outcome of it! Instead of becoming a great and mighty king, and, in war, conquering the whole world, I was going to spend my whole existence shut up in this dreary house, with people who could not comprehend my language any better than I did theirs.

I chafed and grew restless under this thought, and in thinking of it, appeared to grow more stupid every day.

Finally I found a messenger, a friend of mother's, by whom I sent word to her to send a posse of men, under the disguise of messengers, to take me away from the mission by stealth. Would she consent to this or would she lack courage or love to grant my request? I waited impatiently. When the day dawned when the messengers were to come, I wonder I did not excite the suspicion of my teacher, for I was so uneasy, and so little self-contained.

They arrived, not a posse, as I had grandly asked for, but a half-dozen stout, able-bodied men. As usual I went to see them. It was growing dark (they had purposely waited till dusk), and under the cover of darkness they bore me away. I was taken to a village belonging to my mother, and hidden in a hut in the thickest part of the woods. I hoped father would not think of me as a runaway, and thus search for me throughout the kingdom, but think I had made away with my life, as I had threatened at the mission I would do, if not allowed to go home. The news came to him, however, that I had left the mission, presumably with the messengers. They, I learned afterwards, were called up before father, and upon denying all knowledge of me and my whereabouts, were promptly put in the stocks and severely punished.

He had my mother brought before him. She was very calm, and said she knew nothing of me. If he had known the part she had taken in my flight her fate would have been similar to that of the men whom she had employed; but she was so cool and persistent in denying all knowledge of my hiding place that she disarmed any suspicion that he might have had of her.

As day after day wore on, and the searchers he had sent out to scour the woods between Bendoo and the mission returned without me, he became very much enraged at the thought that a boy could outwit him in such a manner, and set his laws at defiance. He was determined to find me, dead or alive.

He sent out a proclamation through the different towns of his territory, running like this :—

Any party or parties having my son Besolow in their possession or harbored in their territory, are hereby given notice that they will be allowed four days to either return him to me at Bendoo, or give me notice of his whereabouts. If at the end of that time the said party or parties do not obey the command conveyed in this message, they will sacrifice their lives.

Signed, KING ARMAII, Bendoo, Upper Guinea.

This proclamation was heralded over all the provinces by a messenger. You know, my dear reader, that I have told you before that the Veys and Mandingoes have a written alphabet, and they are the only ones. There may be other tribes who have, but they are unknown to me.

If mother had been discovered in sheltering me in her village, her death would have followed suddenly and ignominiously. She put me in charge of about two hundred and fifty valiant men of her tribe, and sent us word of the proclamation which father had sent out. She advised us to keep to the thickest, densest part of the woods till the excitement of my disappearance should have blown over.

We obeyed her commands, keeping in the very heart of the forest; and in spite of the danger of capture hanging over our heads, had a very jolly time of it. We lived on bananas and oranges and the game which we killed; and I was constantly comparing the grand freedom and enjoyment of such a life with the narrowness and discomfort of the life at the mission, which at that time I hated most bitterly.

After a week's comparative safety, we heard the sound of bugles and hunting calls in the woods, and knew that traces of our whereabouts had been discovered, and the men were on our track. We evaded our pursuers for two days, but at last met. They numbered about two hundred men; but they were some of the strongest and ablest in father's army. While the front ranks were engaged in fighting, an old chief spirited me away; but we had not gone very far before we were captured. I was bound hand and foot, though I fought against it like a wild-cat, and scratched and bit in a manner that was not stopped till superior strength and chastisement overcame me. Leaving the men fighting in the heart of the forest, several of father's old chiefs bore me off to Bendoo. When I was brought before father, bound hand and foot, and hungry, I expected he would be very angry, and would have my head struck off immediately. He only stood and regarded me with a smile of amusement on his face, and asked me if I had enjoyed my recreation. He said he would put an end to my life, only he knew that the greater punishment would be to have me return to the mission. The teachers should have the power to punish me in any way they might think best, for running away. He did not allow me to see mother, but had me sent, bound as I was, back to "Cape Mount." I think he rather admired my pluck in running away, and the aptness I showed in keeping out of the way of his searchers for so long a time. It was morning when I was brought back to the mission. Mrs. Roberts received me as if nothing had happened, and when the straps were cut from my wrists and ankles, led me into the house, into the white, bare schoolroom, and in the most matter-of-fact way placed an alphabet card in my hand. I had half an idea that my flight and all that attended it must have been a dream, things at the mission flowed on so evenly, and with the same monotonous regularity. Eat, study, eat, study, eat, bed. No one made any remarks on my absence, or took any notice of my return. Yes, it was some days before I could accustom myself to the idea that all that had happened in the last weeks was not a dream, but stern reality. I made up my mind that stay I would not, and at the very first opportunity away I went again. This time I made my way, with surprising rapidity and accurateness, to my father's big warehouse on the coast. I have explained it to you—a large house, forty by fifty feet long. Here the ships from this country and from England landed their freight of goods; and stored at this station, also, were all the goods they would be apt to take away in exchange for what they had brought.

I went to the home of one of father's interpreters and begged for food and shelter. I told her I had run away from the mission, where I was very unhappy, and begged her to shelter me. She was a kind-hearted woman, and without knowing whom she was sheltering, put me in a little room upstairs and left me. I gazed out of the tiny window at the blue, bright ocean, dotted here and there with white sails, and as I gazed my imagination took another flight. I thought of the word America, as I had oftentimes heard it spoken. Where was America? Over the blue, dancing, sunlit waters lay the wonderful home of the white people. Why shouldn't I go there? If my father was determined to keep me among white people, why not go directly to their country, and see the manner in which they lived when at home? I could see there the king of whom Curtis had spoken to me once—Jesus Christ. There was no irreverence in these boyish thoughts. They were wild and ignorant, but earnest and honest enough. To get to America I would only have to go aboard one of those big ships, I supposed. There is no knowing what I should have done if the next morning Mr. Roberts had not put in an appearance. He had traced me to the coast, and soon found me out.

I asked him if he were going to whip me. He assured me not that time, but for the future I must remain tied, and I did remain tied ; but even then I seemed determined to have my freedom, and several times afterwards gnawed the rope in two which bound me, and took to my heels. I do not wonder that they finally lost all patience with me, and thrashed me soundly for every misdemeanor that I committed. I was enough to try the patience of Job. I would not study, and a whole year passed before I had mastered the alphabet, so that I could say it with any degree of rapidity and accuracy. When, at length, I *did* succeed in mastering it I felt as proud and vain as a peacock, and asked permission to go home and exhibit my knowledge to my people.

Leave of absence was granted to me. I believe the teachers didn't care much whether I ran away or not. I half think they would have been glad and thankful to be rid of me. But I did not run off; I went directly as I could to Bendoo. I showed father the permit given me by Mrs. Roberts, and told him that I had been taught all she could teach me, and I actually thought it was the truth.

He was as proud of me as I was proud of myself. "In one year," he said, "when some boys I know have been studying at it for six and seven years and do not know it yet, you have

learnt all there was. O Besolow, I 'm proud of you, my son.
Speak to me in English."

I rattled off the whole alphabet. He looked bewildered.
I guess he thought I knew a great deal. Every time he spoke
a phrase or two of his extremely limited English, I would reply
by saying a number of the letters. Father appeared to be very
much troubled that he could not make out anything I said,
and would ask me in African what I meant, and I would tell
him I could not explain in African. I got along well enough
till I met Curtis, and he very soon undeceived father as to my
knowledge of the language. He told him that I knew nothing
about English, and if he wished me to know something of it, he
had better send me back to the mission ; and, like a bad penny,
back I went. I felt more reconciled after my return this time,
and gave no more trouble then about running away. I became
intimate with a young man somewhat older than I was, Arma
by name, whose father had sent him from Socoto, on my father's
advice. He was a very bright boy, and was only a week, or
perhaps two, in thoroughly learning the alphabet, and went on
rapidly, soon being able to read little words and utter little
phrases. I think the missionaries disliked me, because of my
stupidity and dullness ; and for the opposite qualities in Arma,
they admired and made much of him.

I *was* dull ; I could not keep my mind concentrated on my
lessons. It seemed to be of no use to try. It would wander
away from the subject on hand to the rich, tropical forests, and
to gay dancers, feasts, and games of my people. I could
memorize nothing, and Mrs. Roberts told me afterwards that
she thought at the time that my case was well-nigh hopeless.

Arma was a great source of comfort to me ; for when all the
others on the mission had lost interest in me, he stuck to me
nobly, and gave me many an idea, and much help on some of
the lessons that seemed, ah ! so difficult to me. I was taught,
as I believe young children are taught in this country, by means
of objects. Mrs. Roberts would draw the picture of a cat, and
then pronounce the name over and over again until we had finally
become familiar with the sound of the three letters. Then she
would write it on the board, and we would learn to spell and
pronounce it.

For the others in the class it would be no great task ; but
alas ! unfortunate Besolow. I would stand in front of the board

all day long, gaze at the picture, spell over the letters to myself dozens and dozens of times, with no result whatever save
the result of appearing duller than ever in comparison with the
others.   They came at last to think it not so much a lack of
mental power as it was stubborness and taciturnity on my part;
and they began to punish me, and hold me up to ridicule in
every way.   It was not stubborness, and it was a cruel way to
take, hoping to have better things of me.   I was not allowed
to go to the table when the rest did ; but ate after they did, and
ate what they left.   I was locked into my room every Saturday,
and was not allowed to hunt and frolic with the others ; and the
whippings I got may not be numbered.   It is not to be wondered at much that under such harsh treatment I did not
improve, but seemed to grow more backward every day.

Mrs. Roberts would call Arma and myself to her side, and
would utter simple phrases to us in English, and ask us for the
interpretation in African.   I would never get it correct ; but
Arma would in nine cases out of ten, for which quickness he
would be allowed a half-holiday ; while I would remain behind,
and kept standing in a corner, on one leg, for many hours.
That was a favorite mode that Mrs. Roberts had in which to
punish me.

Instinctively feeling that I was disliked, I became very
melancholy ; and I believe if it had not been for Arma, I
should have made away with myself.   He would talk to me,
and help me, and advise me, and I learned to love him fondly.
Under his tuition, given at spare moments, I began to pick up
a little ; and suddenly the mists seemed to clear away from my
brain, and the little things that had once appeared so difficult
now seemed simple and easy enough.

After this it was quite wonderful, when compared to my
former bluntness, how quickly and readily I mastered the little
lessons which I had from day to day.

In the second year I could study as well as Arma himself,
and before the year had advanced very far, I had equaled
him in many things.   I could interpret the little phrases now
that Mrs. Roberts said over to us, with a proficiency that
delighted me as nothing else ever did ; for what thing can give
us more pleasure than to feel that a heretofore unknown tongue
is becoming our own.   All her interest came back to Mrs.
Roberts as I improved.

I began to read in little primers words of one syllable, most of them being Biblical stories, in which I was very much interested. In an indirect way she began to tell me a little about Jesus Christ, our Saviour; but the idea of his being a man and king, implanted in my mind by Curtis, could not be displaced easily. I had many religious pictures to look at, and thought them pictures of places and people in America. It was not then that the ideas Mrs. Roberts meant to convey to my mind took root.

In the third year I could read very well indeed, and in addition began the study of penmanship. The Bible stories began to awaken much interest in my heart. Mrs. Roberts worked with me very earnestly. I had acquired a great fondness for study, and learned my catechism without much trouble.

She found it a very difficult thing to convince me that our god worship was a wicked thing. I told her to hush, or she might bring some horrible plague upon the mission; and always, after she had talked in this manner, I would creep away by myself, and in some isolated place would offer to the gods some thing, and beg of them to forgive Mrs. Roberts, who was a white person, and did not know what she was saying.

My father came to see me once. He appeared much older, and said he was having a hard time, being obliged to fight off tribe after tribe who were attempting to settle on his territory. At his words I felt all my old-time longing for a warrior's life flare back into my heart, that of late had been filled with the fresh delight of study. But he said no; I would please him best by staying quietly at the mission and becoming a good scholar.

He told me that my brother, who had gone to England, had returned to Bendoo a bright man, but a confirmed drunkard; and a month or so after I heard of his death, caused from the effects of too much rum.

"Don't you disappoint me, Besolow," were father's last words, as I bade him good-bye for the last time.

CHAPTER XII.

WEARY WANDERING.

"Return we could not, nor continue where we were; to shift our place was to exchange one misery with another."—*Stanley*, "*In Darkest Africa.*"

" There is purpose in pain ;
Otherwise it were devilish. I trust in my soul
That the great Master Hand which sweeps over the whole
Of this deep harp of life, if at moments it stretch
To shrill tension some one wailing nerve, means to fetch
Its response, the truest, most stringent, and smart,
Its pathos the purest from out the wrung heart,
Whose faculties, flaccid it may be, if less
Sharply strung, sharply smitten, had failed to express
Just the one note the great final harmony needs."
                                        —*Owen Meredith.*

"My spirit cries, ' Thy will be done ! '
And finds the victory won."—*Theodore Tilton.*

THE LIGHT IS FOUND.

I BEGAN to feel a great interest in the Bible stories, and liked to listen to them when told by Mrs. Roberts or some of the teachers ; but when they told me that Jesus Christ was not a living, human, earthly king, but the blessed Son of the Lord God, I got completely beyond my depth in reasoning upon their words. I thought it complete foolishness. I thought God could not have a son, and yet both be one in the same person ; and it was a wonder to me how these otherwise sensible people could believe any such nonsense.

Here, again, Arma went ahead of me, and with surprising ease grasped and made his own what cost me a long, hard struggle to possess. It was surprising with what tenacity I clung to my old religious ideas, often offering sacrifices to the gods of my people, unbeknown to the missionaries.

The kind teachers used to say, " Besolow, I have come from many, many miles away to try to help you get into the light." "I can see very well," I would make answer; "my eyes are good, I can see as well as you can."

One day when my teacher shook her head, I illustrated the point to her, and endeavored to show her that I spoke truthfully. I put a tiny bead on the table before which she was working. "Can you see that?" I inquired. "Why, yes," she replied. "So can I; I see it also," I made answer. "So you see my eyes are quite strong and well." "Light" had no other significance to me for some time.

They had little if any difficulty in teaching me of God. I could easily conceive of a Supreme Being, and gradually I began to feel that my people's mode of worshiping was needless, if not wicked.

All this was very gradually accomplished, however, but I thought them not in their right minds when they spoke of Christ, the Holy Spirit, and God being distinct powers, but united so that they were one.

They let me alone for a short time, and did not try to teach me of the Trinity till I became more conversant with the language. Here, again, was Arma my friend. He often talked to me of Christ, and as long as he spoke of the earthly man I would listen with much eagerness; but as soon as he spoke of him as God, I lost interest and became incredulous; but Arma persisted, till at length I had a little more faith that what he and the missionaries were telling me of Christ might be true. My faith was, however, very weak and vacillating, and worth but very little to me or to anybody else.

It was no wonder if the missionaries grew impatient, at times. It must have been very discouraging not to see any good fruit springing from their hard efforts to convert me, and from the seed they had worked to plant in my savage breast.

At last Mrs. Roberts said to me, one day: "Besolow, you are wicked. After all I and the others in the mission have told you of His sweet and loving kindness to man, His noble generosity in dying to save us, how can you still refuse to believe in our dear Lord, Jesus Christ? There is Arma, your close friend; see what a good Christian boy he has become. You are wicked, Besolow."

Her words troubled and pained me a good deal. I was not a liar, deceiver, nor traitor, nor scandalmonger, and being free from these faults, why, I had a perfect right to consider myself a righteous man, which I was not slow in doing.

I came to the conclusion, after a great many dreary months had passed, that Christ must be an American God, and a very powerful one as well, because so many intelligent people could believe in him and revere him as they did. But why did they not offer sacrifices to him, as we did? Not human offerings, for they considered those wicked, but sacrifices of the lower animals. This God, if he were a powerful one, ought to be pleased. With redoubled vigor I then studied the catechism, feeling that by so doing I was pleasing the Unknown One. I studied this catechism and the Bible for hours and hours at a time. My teachers were much encouraged, and I said no word to them of my new conception of Christ.

The fact that I was pleasing the American God by studying my lessons well, was a constant impetus to me, and I began to do wonderfully well in my classes.

I entered into all my work with a zest that delighted my instructors ; but all their conversation concerning the plan of salvation made no impression on me whatever. As you American people would say, " It went into one ear and came out the other."

My two dearest prides in life were the suit of civilized clothing which I wore, and wouldn't have parted with for anything else in the world, and my ability for learning the language that I was rapidly beginning to adore.

How discouraged my good friend, Mrs. Roberts, was when she learned at last of my idea of Christ ! I can see her big, dark eyes now, as they were that morning, surcharged with the disappointed tears. " Ah, Besolow," she said, " I expected such fine things of you. I thought you would be a pioneer on the side of our Saviour, and go among your people teaching them of Him. He is not the dear Lord of America alone. He is the sweet Friend of all people, everywhere ; as much the Father of your people as he is of mine. O Besolow, for my sake won't you try to believe? Indeed, indeed, I'm telling you true. Did I not come from far across the waters just to tell you of the good tidings? Pray, pray constantly, Besolow. Ask Him to help your unbelief. Will you do this for my sake ?" And I answered in the affirmative.

Much, and seriously, and often did this kind lady talk to me. She seemed inspired ; and, indeed, I think she was. Arma, also, talked to me a great deal in his own peculiar way ; and, thank

God, the time came when the old, barbarous, uncivilized thoughts and ideas became supplanted by serious, deep ones, such as I had never had in my whole life before.

Were the words of these people true? Were they indeed? Was Jesus Christ the Son of God, yet equal to His Father? Had he really died for me—to save me from sin—he, the Son of God—for *me*—a poor African savage? Did he love and watch over me—and could belief in his power to save prevent me from suffering eternal tortures in Cayanpimbi, and permit me to enjoy forever the peace and rest of Igenie? Words, as I have explained to you, my dear reader, synonymous with Hell and Heaven.

These questions haunted me night and day. I could not get them out of my mind for a moment of time. I spoke to few, heard but few remarks that others made, lost my appetite, neglected my books, as I went about with downcast eyes, pondering over the mighty questions. A camp meeting was held in a distant part of the mission by missionaries who intended going farther into the interior, and Mrs. Roberts persuaded me to go with her. Never shall I forget that time. I sat with the kind lady, my hand clasped warmly in hers, my eyes bent persistently on the ground, as if I would read the answer to my questions in the tiny brown grassblades.

I was very much impressed by the spirited singing and the earnest prayers they offered up, and for me, as Mrs. Roberts asked them to do. I could not but notice, uninitiated as I was, the beautiful rest and peace that seemed to fill the breasts of these Christian people. The meeting lasted for many days, and we remained there during all that time. Ah, how weary and heavy-laden I was! I was more miserable than I care to remember. My heart was bursting with a longing for something, I knew not what.

"Besolow," said Mrs. Roberts, "do you want to believe on Jesus Christ, your Lord and Saviour?"

"Yes, yes," I answered eagerly, as joyous hymn after joyous hymn stirred the forest to its depth ; "yes, Mrs. Roberts, but I cannot."

"Pray, my dear brother," she answered. "Kneel down and pray to God these words : 'I wish to believe on Christ; help my unbelief.'" Dear Mrs. Roberts! God bless her! She was a tender friend to me at that period of my life. I do not know how I should have gotten along without her. She was loving and sympathetic as a mother.

She understood my case far better than I did myself. She knew that often before the glorious presence and light of Jesus Christ visited the human soul, it very often seemed lost in a chaos of darkness and despair; and she told me of this. For hours and hours I would kneel with bowed head and repeat these words, "Dear Jesus, help my unbelief"—say them over and over again, till my tired lips refused to utter them; then I would say them mentally, till the tissues of my brain would refuse to act, and oftentimes I fainted from sheer exhaustion,— "Dear Jesus, help my unbelief."

"Is it brighter, Besolow?" Mrs. Roberts asked often.

"No, no," I would cry out in despair; "the darkness is blacker than ever."

"Poor boy! poor Besolow! Have patience, and all will yet be well."

She would pray with me: "O dear Father who art in heaven, cast down thy all-pitying, all-loving eye upon this kneeling boy, who does desire so fervently, beloved Jesus, to become one of your own sanctified ones. Have pity upon him, and let the beautiful radiance of thy dear presence chase away the gloom that surrounds his soul." While she prayed I said over my one little prayer, "Help my unbelief!" till it seemed branded in words of fire on my brain. I cannot help but wonder if many people suffer as I did before they find their precious Saviour.

One day, feeling a strong desire for solitude, I crept away by myself to the woods, here to pray and to weep, and to call upon the unknown God to help me in the sorrow of which my undisciplined brain could not define the cause. As I knelt in supplication, a large yellow snake crawled over my legs, and disappeared in some thick foliage at my right. I cowered down in affright; for I, poor, ignorant, superstitious boy, took it for a sign that this God, Christ, to whom I was praying, was displeased with me. I returned to the camp meeting more wretched than ever.

I would not partake of any food, thinking that if I maintained a rigid fast, Christ would reveal himself to me. As day followed day, many of the missionaries would come and kneel beside me, and ask me if there was any change in my mind or heart.

"No, no, no," I would tell them, lifting my hollow eyes to their faces pleadingly; "and I do not believe there ever will be."

They comforted me and prayed with me, with slight, if any satisfactory result; and I went on with my little prayer, "Help my unbelief." Some days, fainting for the want of food and drink, my feet would refuse to support my body, and I would fall weakly to the ground. I was in despair, for in spite of my fasting and praying, I was apparently as far from the blessed state described by the missionaries as ever.

At the expiration of almost every minute I would look at my hands, my fingers, my body, to see if any radical change were taking place; for, poor, illiterate fellow as I was, I believed that a "change" meant a physical transformation of some kind.

May those who read this little book never know what it means to suffer as I did in the month that followed. Only for the thoughtfulness and kindness of Mrs. Roberts and the others, I do not believe I could have lived.

Yes, it was for one long, awful month that in this fashion I struggled to find Christ. And one day—ah, beautiful day! the fairest in my life—I was kneeling, as usual, my kind friend by my side. With all my soul in the words, I said after her: "I yield, I give myself wholly, to Thee. Take me, O Jesus, all crime-stained as I am, and make Thy Spirit felt within me. I love Thee; I trust Thee; help Thou my unbelief."

My Christian friends will understand what followed; will understand the indescribable joy that filled my soul at that moment! Oh! the effulgent, glorious light that seemed to fill my heart and mind! The great, lovely uplifting of soul; the completeness of a longed-for, indefinable joy that seemed to meet my every want; the delight of "the peace that passeth all understanding"; the exquisite sensation of a nearness to my Saviour! It was all like a joy that kills from its very intensity. It proved too much for my weak, frail body, and with the happy tears pouring from my eyes, I fell prone upon my face, unconscious. When I came to myself I was lying on a knoll of thick, sweet-smelling grass, under the shade of a tree; the missionaries were singing in the distance, and Mrs. Roberts was sitting beside me.

"Is it well with thee, my brother?" she asked, tenderly.

Well! Ah, I had no words in my slight vocabulary to describe the peace that had fallen on my life! Now I could partake of food with a relish, and pray and sing with the others with a renewed life and ardor; for all the old misery of doubt and gloom had been lifted from my heart, and I felt free and happy as the birds of the air. When I returned to the mission I worked very hard over the Bible; especially dear to me was Isaiah, in the Old Testament, and John iii. 16 in the New. I learned to love the books that told so much of Him, the blessed One.

Mrs. Roberts had no difficulty now in arousing my interest in the precious Word, and very soon I became the best Bible student on the mission. She talked to me a good deal about my future. We were sitting on the piazza together; she was sewing and I was at her feet, with an open book on my lap, from which I was studying at the odd moments when we were not conversing. "Besolow," she said, "very soon now you will go back to your people. Do you think that when you are with them once again, you will forget your Lord, and fall back into your old ways of worshiping idols?" I looked up at her without a word, and she must have read in my eyes the rebuke I did not speak, for she reached over towards me and laid her hand ever so gently on my head.

"Forgive me, brother," she said, "if I have caused you pain; but I couldn't help but wonder if you would always be true. It will be very hard to keep your faith, may be, when you are away from here. You might possibly, among your own people, be ashamed or afraid to stand up for Jesus. But remember He was not ashamed nor afraid to die for you."

"You need have no fear, dear Mrs. Roberts," I made answer. "I will never refuse to acknowledge what a friend I have found in Christ. Indeed, of late, one thought has taken possession of me and haunts me all the time, and that is, the necessity of my people—the Vey people—knowing of Him whose blood can take away the sins of the world! Once I used to think I would like to be a great warrior and hunter; but now I would rather be His disciple than anything else in the world."

"Good! I am overjoyed to hear you talk so; all my trouble is repaid many times over; and do not forget these words you have said to me, Besolow, when you go back among your people.

It is yours to do great good for your people, remember. Be true to your convictions."

"It is yours to do great good for your people." I have never forgotten those words, and never shall, for I intend to live up to them as long as I live.

Arma's father withdrew him from the mission. I was very sad at his departure. We had a long talk before he went away, and he strongly advised me to go into mission work, and declared that he was going to work in that field. Dear Arma ! I have never seen him since, but I know that if he is alive, Africa is the better for his living in it. He was a remarkably bright, enthusiastic, Christian young man. Mrs. Roberts felt sorry to lose him, for by precept and example he had been a great help in training the young, raw savages who came and went to the mission.

I fell into his place when he left, and filled it to the satisfaction of those about me. As I stood over some lonely African boy, and pointed out to him the different letters on a pasteboard alphabet card, my mind would travel back to the time when I myself had so much difficulty with the thing. Perhaps, remembering it, I had more patience with the backward boys than ever Mrs. Roberts had with me, or would have had with them. Be that as it may, they got along nicely under my tuition, and Mrs. Roberts was fond of praising me for their progress. I must confess I did enjoy her praises as much as I was hurt at her censure, which was seldom given at that time.

Among all the boys, I think I was her favorite ; I think she cared most for me. "Do you remember, Mrs. Roberts," I asked her one day, "how much you used to dislike me?" The color crept into her cheeks. "No, Besolow," she answered, "I never disliked you, but you were a hard case to manage. Who would have thought you would have grown to be such a fine young man?"

"I *was* stupid," I admitted, "and willful, and wild. There is no need of tying me here now. I have no desire to leave the mission. It seems to me like a home."

"I am glad to hear you say so," she said, with her kindly smile.

I was somewhat distressed in mind just then by the news brought me by the messengers. A war was being threatened between my father and a very powerful king of a neighboring tribe ; cause, the same old one,—disputed territory. I hoped father would not enter into the engagement, for I had a foreboding that if he did he would lose his life. I knew the tribe with which he anticipated a battle to be an exceedingly strong and powerful one, and father had lost a great many men in recent skirmishes, and was not properly equipped for war just at that time.

Then, besides this fact, the messengers whom he sent told me that he was not very well, and of late had been much under the care of the medicine-men. He had been suffering, too, along with all the rest, from the petty meanness of my uncle, his brother, a king over a large number of people situated northwest of Vey territory. This brother had always disliked father, and in many little disagreeable ways had tormented and irritated him.

Word came to father at this time that when he went to war uncle intended coming to Bendoo, and taking possession of it. Father did not put much credit in this rumor, it appears ; but I did, and it worried me greatly. I knew uncle to be an unprincipled, as well as a cruel man, who, to serve his own ends, would stop at nothing. I became very much disturbed in my mind, and waited eagerly, week after week, for news from my home. My first temptation came in a message brought me by the men. Father would like to have me come back and enter into the engagement. He did not command me ; I should come or not, as I saw fit, but he needed me, and wished that I would. Ah ! then for a time I forgot all my conversations with, and promises to, Mrs. Roberts. At the thought of another active engagement, with all its attending excitement and dangers, my blood thrilled through my veins, and mounted hotly into my face.

All the old dreams of becoming a famous soldier came back into my heart, and I did not read the "Good Book" as zealously as I had before. I wanted to go back and fight, but I felt ashamed, after my firm promises, to broach the subject to Mrs. Roberts. I thought of it a great deal, and finally the dear lady noticed that something was troubling me, and she questioned me as to what the matter was. I stood before her in silence for a few minutes, and if I had been a white man she would have seen me, what you call, blushing.

"Are you worrying about your father, Besolow?" she queried.

"Yes, Mrs. Roberts."

"Are you alarmed lest he be beaten in this engagement?"

"Yes, Mrs. Roberts."

"Do you think you would like to go back and fight with him?"

I hung my head as I stammered, "Yes, Mrs. Roberts."

She was silent for a little time; then she spoke of the promises I had made about devoting myself to the cause of Christ for the rest of my life, and how I could not do this in the best, most complete way and be a warrior. "This is your first temptation to give up that idea of yours that made me so very happy. Overcome this, and the next one will not be so difficult to master. Remember, too," she said again, "that the bravest, truest soldier on the face of the earth is the Christian soldier. Besolow, as I have told you once before, I have made great sacrifices for Christ's cause. I left the blessed shores of America twenty long years ago; left mother, father, sister, and brother to come to your dark land, and teach your people of the redemption from sin through Christ. Why, I know not, but my efforts have been crowned with poor success. You are the only one whom I have succeeded in converting through my own instrumentality; and now, as I am growing old and feeble, it would break my heart if you did not come up to my expectations. I have great hopes of you. I am going to see what can be done about sending you to America, to obtain a liberal education; and, Besolow, I want you to promise a weak-minded woman, who has your interest much at heart, that you will preach the gospel to your people after obtaining a thorough education; that you, an African yourself, will give your life to the African cause."

She put out her hand, and I took it in mine, humbly. How much this little, weak woman had done for me and mine! She had labored far away from home and friends, and familiar modes of living, for twenty long years. I was much impressed with her nobility of mind and heart, and promised her for the second time, on my word of honor, to do as she wished me to do; and, thank God, I have never forgotten that promise, and it is towards its best fulfillment that I am tending day by day—working, studying, and planning for it—keeping it fresh before my eyes as if it were given yesterday.

So when father's messengers came back, I told them I wished him success, but I did not care to take any part in the battle myself. I thought they looked somewhat disappointed ; and now I waited in a fever of suspense to hear the result.

It was as I feared ; after a long, hard battle, my father's forces, greatly lessened, were defeated, and father himself seriously wounded. At the news I felt my old savage nature rise into arms again, and cry out for vengeance on the tribe that had maimed my father. It was only by constant and continual prayer that I was pacified, and my fiery nature calmed.

Father felt that his death was near, and expressed a desire to see me. Mrs. Roberts readily granted me permission, and I set out for Bendoo.

CHAPTER XIII.

" Thou who comest from on high,
  Who all woes and sorrows stillest,
Who for twofold misery,
  Hearts with twofold balsam fillest,
Would this constant strife would cease!
  What are pain and rapture now?
Blissful peace,
  To my bosom hasten thou!"—*Goethe.*

THE LAND OF THE FREE.

" The land which freemen till,
  Which sober-suited freedom chose;
A land where, girt with friends or foes,
A man may speak the thing he will."—*Tennyson.*

WEARY WANDERING.

UPON my arrival in Bendoo I was greeted with music, and dancing, and bonfires; but on a very quiet scale compared to the usual clamor and hullabaloo employed in ceremonies of welcome. My boy friends were glad to see me, and crowded around me, asking question after question concerning the white people and the mission I had left. I gave them a few ideas as briefly as I could. My appearance had filled the young fellows with the greatest consternation and wonder, for I wore the full outfit of civilized men; they circled about me as if I had been some curious animal, and asked me the use of this article of clothing and the need of that, till they very nearly drove me distracted. My appearance seemed to strike some of them in a ridiculous light, and they rolled over and over on the ground in paroxysms of laughter. One begged to put on my coat; another tried on my hat, and went capering about with it on his head; and others were kneeling at my feet, closely examining my boots. To say the least this was very disagreeable; but I knew that it would not be policy to resent it, as I felt like doing. Finally I got them quieted and subdued by showing them my watch, which was a Waterbury, the first they had ever seen. They crowded eagerly about me, asking me more questions about it than I could answer. It passed from hand to hand, and they all examined it and commented upon it with the delight and interest of little children.

"Now talk some English to us, Besolow," they said. "Talk to us in English." "Good-morning," I said blandly. This had the effect of sending the humorous ones off into another fit of laughter; and then I went on saying in English all the little phrases of which I could think. They made me interpret all that I could for them. "It is hard, and not beautiful like our own language," said one of them. "I do not like it; I never want to learn the English." I grew tired, at length, of posing before them as somewhat of a curiosity, and gaining possession of my various articles of clothing which they had been examining, I went to my mother's hut. She was seated just inside the door, embroidering a long, crimson silk robe, meant, I suppose, for one of the priests. At first she did not know me, but stared in wonderment at me, marveling at the oddity of my apparel. Then with a sudden, delighted cry she threw aside her work and sprang into my arms.

"Besolow," she exclaimed, joyfully, "my son! I see you once again!" We spent a very happy hour together. In that hour I spoke to her of my life at the mission, and also of Jesus Christ. Poor mother! She was much bewildered; but when she finally realized that I was speaking to her of a God of whom she knew nothing, she glanced fearfully about the room, and then went and kindled a little fire before the shrine of the household god. "Oh, my son," she said, "what have these people done! Changed your ideas in regard to our gods? Do not, as you value your life, let this be known to the medicine-men. Oh, woe! woe! woe!" She began to rock herself backwards and forwards in a passion of grief and regret, that seemed altogether pitiful to me; for how could I ever hope to eradicate the faith of a lifetime, and teach this poor, dark soul of Him whose name is synonymous with "Light?" I comforted her as best I could, and changed the subject by asking after father. This only had the effect of causing the tears to flow the faster. "He will die," she said; "he is suffering much pain. Woe to our people! Woe to Vey on the day he dies!"

"Hush, mother," I said; "how gloomily you talk. My elder brother, Solobey, is a brave, strong, bright man, and he will take father's place, and govern as wisely and well as he did."

"Nay, nay, Besolow; it will not be so. I consulted the gods last night, and they said to me: 'Woe! Devastation and bloodshed! Devastation, bloodshed, and woe! woe! woe! to the people of Vey.'"

In spite of myself I felt a feeling of superstition take possession of me as mother's weird voice and piteous words rang through the little room. That evening I went to see father. He was dying,—even my unpracticed eye could see that much,—and he was suffering violent pain.

To us death-throes have a material and strange significance. The dying man is on one bank of a dark and gloomy river, and is struggling to reach the opposite bank, whereon all is bright, and happy, and peaceful. His spirit has a hard struggle to get to Igenie. Every long breath and restless movement of the body served to show the onlookers just what a struggle it is having. The body it is that·is holding back the spirit. They say my father's death agonies were pitiful to behold; and at last the medicine-man declared that he would free the spirit from the encumbering body, and he, as is the custom of my people, advanced to the side of the couch and cut my father's throat. The body was quiet, and they drew sighs of satisfaction as they spoke, in subdued tones, of the happy arrival of the struggling spirit to Igenie. It all seemed very horrible and barbarous to me; but I made no remarks upon the custom then.

After father was laid out in state, and his body anointed with oils and ointments, and arrayed in his finest habiliments, songs were chanted over him mournfully, and many of his wives came forward desiring to be buried alive with him. This is considered to be the highest honor that can be conferred upon a woman,—burial with her husband,—especially if he be chief or an officer of some rank. In this instance one of the best-looking was selected. She was clad in a long tunic of white silk, which had been sent from Europe, and wore on her arms and neck gaudy jewelry. She looked as if she were decked out for a bride, instead of the cruel fate in store for her. "Lebe," they said, "pause and consider awhile before you give up your life in this manner." "I am happy," she said; and to all their remonstrances she made the self-same response, "I am happy." Nothing could dissuade her from the foolish and horrible step she was about to take. When father was lowered into the grave, she was placed in after him. Over the grave was placed a boat-shaped wooden arrangement filled with sharp spikes. The longest and sharpest of these spikes were placed directly over the woman's head.

A squadron of soldiers stood at the right; at a given command they fired as one man; and as the report of their guns died away, this spiked wood was forced down, down, till one violent scream from the woman told the spikes had penetrated her brain. This wicked custom is a common one among my race, and a man is seldom buried that a woman does not sacrifice herself in this way. Indeed, as I have said before, she deems it a great honor and glory to be allowed to do so. Immediately after father's burial, and very much against mother's will, I returned to the mission. Mrs. Roberts was very glad to see me. I told her that my eldest brother, Solobey, a fine boy, was to be king in father's place, and so it had been arranged. I told her I would strive with all my might to convert him to Christianity. My words had the effect of making the dear lady very happy. Alas for the frailty of man's plans!—it was not more than two weeks after my return to the mission, that news came to me that my uncle had invaded father's territory with many hundreds of men, usurped the throne, and was governing the people with an iron will and merciless hand; so much so, in fact, that they were completely cowed, and made no resistance. My mother's children were the rightful heirs to father's possessions, because she was the wife of highest birth. I had three elder brothers, all of whom bitterly resented uncle's course.

Before I learned of his treachery he dispatched a messenger for me, with great offerings of love and friendship, and asking for my presence in Bendoo. Happily I learned of his plans in time. A messenger in whom he had confided, but who had some feelings left in his breast, told me that he intended to leave no stone unturned till he had put me to death, and then everything would be clear before him; he would be rightful heir to all my father's estates, and no one could gainsay him. I was very anxious to return to my native town to see what changes were taking place, and to use all my influence and power to dethrone this wicked man if I could. By night, stealthily disguised in a manner to baffle discovery, I reached Bendoo again. I walked about the dear old town, where so

many of my boyhood's happy days had been spent; and saw,
as I kept thinking, for the last time, the old friends, bowed,
humbled, and crest-fallen. They knew me not. I crept to the
neighborhood of my mother's hut. Alas! it was occupied by
a new tenant; and the shrill voice of one of my uncle's wives
reached my ears as I lingered. I dared not remain till daybreak, lest he should discover and put me to death. Where
should I go? There was no one now to pay for me at the
mission, and I was too proud to go back there on the charity
of the dear friends who were far from being rich, as I well
knew; so, sore-hearted and miserable, I went out among the
towns on the outskirts of the Vey provinces. Ah, my friends,
for some pages, now, must I dwell upon a life whose miseries
are not experienced by many, I hope. I would not like to
think that many of my fellow-men are suffering as I suffered
for the several ensuing months.

I dared not confess my identity to any one, for, parsimonious
and grasping as I knew them to be, I felt certain that they
would be only too glad to betray me to my uncle for a small
quantity of gold-dust, to say nothing of getting installed into
his good graces by the action. I had a new experience then:
for the first time in my life, but not for the last, I was penniless
and friendless. I slept in the woods, and killed all the small
game I could with a large stick, for I had no spear or cutting
implement of any kind.

I dared not remain long in one place, lest the people might
suspect and acquaint my uncle of my whereabouts; and I got
into a part of the territory—the most remote part—where the
forests were few, and the game correspondingly limited. What
was I to do? I stole an axe as I went through one of the
towns. With this axe I cut wood, and carrying it on my head
for two and three miles at a time, exchanged it for the food
necessary to sustain my body. At times, when a man or a
town was distinguished for thrift, they would not buy my wood,
preferring to cut their own, and then I would often go hungry,
having nothing upon which to subsist, save berries and wild
fruits; the orange and banana did not grow luxuriantly in those
districts. I carried wood in this manner till the top of my head
became soft and sensitive to touch as that of a newly-born
babe. For a long time I struggled on God's beautiful earth
for a mere existence. Many an African native sharper than

his companions, when I approached his door with my wood, would recognize a resemblance between me and his deceased king ; and knowing, perhaps, of the disappearance of the only son from Liberia, would say to me, curiously : "Are you not from Bendoo? Are you not the son of Carttom? I hear that one of his sons is wandering about the country in disguise, in fear of his uncle, who, if he catch him, will put him to death. Are you the man? Tell me, and I will help you." I would deny having ever seen Bendoo, or that I was any relation to the deceased king,—with some pangs from my conscience, it is true,—but I knew these people to be untrustworthy ; I had no faith in their fair promises, and would leave the town as soon as possible, lest they should dispatch a messenger to uncle that I was there. As I journeyed on from place to place in this manner, I heard of Taradobah. She had taken possession of a southern province, and had quite a retinue of soldiers in her train. She was the queen of the province, and as cool-headed, determined, and as much of a warrior as any man (be he ever so strong and valiant) could have been.

She and my uncle hated each other most bitterly. My uncle was a Xerxes-like man. He was tall, finely built, and good to look upon, but weak-minded and crafty. He bought a great quantity of wines and liquors, and gave feast after feast, spending his time in this manner instead of minding the affairs of the territory. Under my father's government the sub-tribes were docile and obedient enough ; but under uncle's control they revolted, and withdrew from under his rule, and he lacked the strength and force of character to subdue them, until now the territory he governs isn't much larger than the State of Rhode Island. As I said before, Taradobah despised my uncle most heartily.

She had tried, upon his entrance into Bendoo, to raise an insurrection among the people ; but he had nipped her plans in the bud, just before they were ready for consummation. Followed by five or six hundred of the warriors in and about Bendoo, she had taken possession of this province ; it was, too, one of the best and richest of all the lands that had been owned by my father, and, naturally enough, uncle wished to possess it. He had sharply commanded her to vacate it ; she sent him back words of hatred and defiance by the messenger whom he had sent. She had strengthened her forces, and the fortifications surrounding the town, and calmly awaited developments. He waged war against this plucky woman in three successive battles, and in each one was ignominiously and disgracefully defeated. She was general over her troops, and herself led them out to the battle, fighting herself with the tenacity and strength of a giantess, and she holds the province to this day. Not only does she still hold this land, but since then she has subdued and conquered many of the surrounding petty chiefs. Apropos—she has a son who is now studying at Central Tennessee College, Momoro.

It may not be strange that in my time of need, destitution, and extremity, my thoughts went out to Taradobah, this remarkable women, who had ever been kind to me in the happy days now gone forever. I determined to make my way to her province, and ask her protection and help. As I made my way to her over mountains and through deep, tangled forests, I often thought of the words she said to me once when I first came home from the school. "Besolow," she had said, "if ever the time comes when you need a friend, come to me and you will find one."

Surely, I thought to myself,—as something very like a sob rose in my breast, and made itself heard over my lips,—surely, if ever I needed a friend I need one now. What if, under these new circumstances in which she was placed, Taradobah should refuse to favor me—refuse even to recognize me? Ah, that would be too cruel! That would be more than I could bear! I asked Christ to put it into her heart to show me kindness, and he answered my prayer, for she treated me with the utmost consideration and respect. When I spoke to her of this, she took my hand.

"Why should I not treat the future king of Vey lands with all the respect that is due him? That is what you are, Besolow, a king; the man who holds the place you ought to fill is a base, mean fellow, and we will oust him from it, and put you where you belong."

She had just succeeded in defeating uncle for the third time, and was feeling considerably elated over it, being pretty sure of her powers to subdue and bend him to her will.

Impulsively I answered her, "Yes." I was so tired, so weary, and so lonely, that I forgot Mrs. Roberts and my promises to her, as I thought of the advantages of occupying the position described by Taradobah. Besides this, I reasoned to myself, as king over my people could I not gradually present the blessed faith of Christianity to them, and in time convert them all to the faith? Surely I was justified in trying to accomplish such an end.

"Your mother's brother, Mornbro, is a very powerful chief," she said, "and he will be willing to help you. He and I will unite forces, and will do all in our power to get your inheritance for you."

I thanked her, and then gladly enough gave myself over to the pleasures she had prepared for me as an honored guest. She could not have shown any more politeness to father had he been alive, and come to visit her. First, she went through a ceremony of crowning me as king. She obliged me to cast aside my old clothing, and don the beautiful flowing coronation robes of scarlet cloth and a tiger-skin, in which I felt very fine and grand indeed. Followed by a long line of chiefs and warriors, I went to the hut of one of her first-rank medicine-men, whom I begged for favor. He came out of the hut and graciously consented to heed my request. He murmured some heathenish words over me. I dropped my head in shame and sorrow, for they were prayers to his gods and idols. Christ was regarding these proceedings. Would he be very much displeased? Would I pain him very much? After all I was working for his cause, and surely, *surely* the end justified the means! "Forgive me," I whispered under my breath; but my conscience was a stern mentor, and never, never slept for an instant of time.

Next, Mr. Medicine-man sprinkled me with a powder, and smeared my face all over with greases and ointments of various kinds. Then tremendous volleys of shot were fired off by the soldiers who were stationed in fine order close by; after which, with much solemnity, Taradobah formally declared me King of Vey. She assisted me to rise from my kneeling position; and then the "reception" was tendered me. A lovely chair of solid ivory that had belonged to father, and of which Tarado-bah had taken possession when she left Bendoo, was set for me; and into this I sank, while all the people of the district circled about me with their drums and clappers, and played and danced to show their respect for me. Frequently the musicians prostrated themselves at my feet, and in the old manner I have described to you, endeavored to show their veneration for me, by beating up the dust in terrific clouds with their hands and feet.

Men came to me beautifully dressed in gay, bright colors, each bearing cases filled respectively with bottles of rum, wine, and whiskey. I knew I was expected to drink three times, partaking of some of each kind of liquor; and I did so. If I did not, I should be committing a breach of etiquette that might never be forgiven me. After this was over, I was shown to a large hut, and left alone till the "feast" was announced. This consisted of a whole roasted lamb.

Etiquette was not observed to any great extent at the common board. We all carved for ourselves, and made not much ado about tearing off parts of the flesh with our hands. I thought of my white friends at the mission, and wondered what they would think of this mode of eating.

Now came the last feature of the day's ceremonies. I was again placed in my ivory chair, and a poor, trembling prisoner was brought up before me. He had been taken from my uncle; and Taradobah, who sat close beside me on a gay rug, seemed to take a cruel delight in anticipating the fate of the poor trembling wretch.

"Taradobah," I said, "will you do me a favor?"

"Yes," she said, kindly.

"Will you spare the life of this wretched man?"

She frowned, and I saw that she did not like my request; but she had promised to grant it, and she did so. I shall never forget the look of gratitude that the prisoner cast upon me as he was led away. "Your mother told me before she died that you had adopted many strange, wild notions while on that mission. If you have, Besolow, I advise you to do one of two things; i. e., go back to the mission where such words will be appreciated, or stay here and think no more of them."

Rapidly and eagerly I told her of Christ. It was not a wild, strange notion, I said; it was the sweetest and best faith under the sun."

"Paugh!" she said, rising, "you will not be here five more days before you will laugh with me at this crazy idea of yours."

I grew very serious. Would I indeed ever forget my Saviour? I thought of Mrs. Roberts then, and all her words of pleading, and all the rest of the day I could not get her from my thoughts.

CHAPTER XIV.   •

" Let music swell the breeze,
And ring from all the trees,
Sweet freedom's song;
Let mortal tongues awake,
Let all that breathe partake,
Let rocks their silence break,
The sound prolong."

—America.

MY STRUGGLE FOR AN EDUCATION.

" Yet I argue not
Against Heaven's hand or will, nor bate a jot
Of heart or hope; but still bear up and steer
Right onward."

—Milton.

"THE LAND OF THE FREE."   •

For three days the matter was given to open discussion in the council, and the leading chiefs of Taradobah's tribe and my uncle's decided to go to war for me. I decided then—and it was the first time I had decided about it, and it cost me many a pang—I decided not to return to Liberia, but to join with my friends in striving to get back the kingdom, also to revenge the cowardly murder of my relatives. No sooner had I made this decision than my mind troubled me greatly. This was a base manner of keeping my word to the good people at the mission. I told myself this over and over again. What kind of a contemptible, lying fellow would they think me, who could break his pledged word thus lightly?

As the war preparations went on busily, I often thought of them; many, many times I grew sad and unhappy, and tried to ease my mind with the thought that I was going to battle for Jesus Christ; for once in my possession, I would plant in the lands of Vey the banner of the Gospel. But these smooth ideas did not deceive my conscience in the slightest. I had worldly interests at heart above all else, and a living, growing desire for vengeance.

Sometimes, as I pondered over these things, the thoughts of the coming war were very distasteful to me. Was I not going to pay evil for evil? and was not that a direct offense against the teachings of Christ? It was about this time that the New York State Colonization Society passed a resolution to educate some of the young men in the provinces that were adjacent to Liberia. I had communicated my whereabouts to Mrs. Roberts, whom I knew would be worried over me, and she forwarded me a letter asking me to come back to her immediately for a little time, as she wished to talk with me on matters of importance. "Besolow," she wrote, "I am very feeble and ill, and may not live much longer. As a last favor I want you to come to me. Do not refuse the last request of, yours in Christ,—ROBERTS."

I could not refuse this request of Mrs. Roberts, and informed Taradobah that I was going to the mission, but would return to her in the course of a few days. She was very much averse to my doing anything of the kind.

"The preparations for war are about ripe," she said, "and I need you; you could not go away in a more critical time, Besolow." I told her of Mrs. Roberts' illness. "She was one of the best friends I ever had, Taradobah, and now that she may be dying, and wants to see me, I must go to her."

"Does she want you to cut her throat? Surely there are plenty of her friends who will do that for her, and loosen the spirit from the body." She had reference to the horrid custom that takes place at dying people's bedsides, and which I have described in a preceding chapter.

"No," I said; "that is a custom which white people do not observe."

I found Taradobah's eyes fixed upon me suspiciously. "You like these white people altogether too well, Besolow; and sometimes I have thought since you came back from them you haven't the proper respect for our gods and ceremonies."

I made her no reply. "Tell me, is it so?" she commanded. For the second time, in my rude, direct way, I spoke to her of Jesus Christ; and for the second time she interrupted me with loud laughter, and warnings to keep my new ideas to myself, if I valued my life. "How," she said, "can you expect the gods to be propitious to you in this engagement if you show them so little respect as to supplant them by a white man's god? The white man's god is all very well, Besolow; but it is the black man's god who understands the black man's needs and wants." I said nothing. The next morning I set out for the mission, promising Taradobah to come back inside of a few days.

My wicked heart smote me when they led me to the bed-side of her who had done so much for my advancement. She was very slight, and white as the pillow upon which her head lay weakly, and I could see that she was very, very sick. At sight of me she stretched out one frail hand, and the tears rolled over her cheeks. "Besolow," she said, "I am so glad you have returned." I knelt down beside her bed, and bowed my head humbly over the hand which I still held in my own.

"Where have you been, Besolow, all these months?" she asked, gently. I told her briefly as I could, keeping back nothing. "Do you remember," she said, "of sitting beside me on the piazza one day many months ago, of the long con-versation we had of your future, and the promises which you made me? Those promises made me very happy, as I told you they did at the time. Are you going to break those prom-ises?" She turned her great, pure eyes upon me, full of pain, and her voice trembled with the intensity of her feelings. I spoke of going to war to forward Christ's cause, etc. "Ah, Besolow, do not deceive yourself; you are going to fight for human benefits, and nothing else. God does not want his cause advanced in any such cruel way as that; it is these constant battles and wars that keep back your race and people from enjoying the light and fullness of civilization. Besolow, for my sake give up this idea, and devote yourself to the cause of Christianity in its highest, most ideal sense. The New York State Colonization Society is willing to help a few of the young men, whom they purpose to educate in America; after their education is completed, they will come back to their country to teach and preach. I have spoken to their agent of you,—oh, Besolow, if you will go !"

I knelt before her in perfect silence, and she did not break it for some time ; then she slipped a Testament from under her pillow and placed it in my hand. "Read," she said, "read it to me." I opened, by chance, at the first chapter of John, and read what I found heavily marked :—

"All things were made by Him ; and without him was not

anything made that was made. In him was life ; and the life was the light of men. And the light shineth in darkness ; and the darkness comprehended it not. . . . He came unto his own, and his own received him not. But as many as received him, to them gave he power to become the sons of God, even to them that believe on his name."

I read on till she told me I had read sufficient ; then I returned the Testament, and rose.

"There is a young Vey man here," she said ; " he has just returned from America, where he graduated from Lincoln University. I want you to see him and talk with him."

She held out her hand to me again, and as I took it, smiled up at me encouragingly. I saw the young man of whom she spoke—a tall, straight young fellow, with bright eyes, and the light of intellect shining upon all his features. He spoke to me of the offer made me by the Colonization Society, and besought me with much earnestness to accept of it, saying that I might never have another such opportunity. He spoke of the good I might do my country, armed for life with a good education. "The future of Africa depends upon the exertions of her own sons—the exertions of her own people. They will do more to revolutionize things in our benighted land than fifty thousand outsiders could do," he said. " In a few years you will come back here, Besolow, with new ideas concerning civilization, an excellent and liberal education, the blessings of which you cannot conceive ; and so will be armed to help our people into the Divine light of the gospel as you could never do now. Think it over, my friend, carefully. Mrs. Roberts has spoken to me about the war in which you are to take part, and the cause of it. Your uncle is as likely to win as you are, and in that case you will be worse off than ever ; and as king of the Vey people, Besolow, you could not do them nearly so much good as would be possible if you were an educated, thoroughly civilized, Christian man."

Carefully enough did I consider the two points of this question,—"To be, or not to be." Whether I should enter into hostilities against my uncle, and attempt to get back my rightful position on my own land, or go to America, a strange, unknown country over the seas, to be educated and civilized.

Good arguments and advice as to the reasons why I should adopt the latter course were brought to bear upon the question by those who were interested in me ; but though I took into grave consideration all they told me, it was Mrs. Roberts who made me see what my duty was ; and it was she who won from me the promise that I would go to America. Her last words were, " Promise me, Besolow, that you will preach the gospel to your people."

"Yes," I answered, while my voice was choked with tears ; "I promise."

I sent word to Taradobah as to what I intended doing. As might be expected, she was very angry, disappointed, and not a little disgusted.

The agent of the Society did not find a great many of the young men who, when it came to the point, would leave their native shores. There were about six of us who remained unchanged, after having finally decided to go. The timid ones tried to throw a wet blanket over our plans.

" You will die," some of them said, " before you ever reach the ' new land.' "

"They are taking you away to kill you," were the comforting words of some of the others. " You will never see your native land again. You had better bear with the dangers and trials of your own land, than ' fly to others which you know not of.' "

But my mind was decided. I knew that never again could I forget my promise to Mrs. Roberts. I was now bent upon obtaining an education, let the cost be what it would ; and the words of the would-be enemies of the cause had no effect on me whatever.

Shall I ever forget the bright, sunlit day upon which I said good-bye to my native land, when I sailed from Monrovia ? I stood on the deck of the vessel and watched the fading shore till it was nothing but a blue, misty film, where the sky and ocean seemed to meet. Blinded with the sorrowful tears which I could not keep back. I sought my room, and prayed fervently for many hours. I kept my room for most of the way, for I became very seasick. The captain treated me most kindly, but day after day I would lie in my bunk and long for death. Was this illness a punishment vented upon me for leaving my native shores ? I banished the thought that harbored a suspicion of my old-time religion and superstition ; but, alas ! it was not mine to banish the pain quite so readily. As we neared our journey's end I began to feel considerably better, and was very much interested in the boat and the gear, spending most of my time on deck.

Can you imagine the amazement of a poor, bewildered African boy, when the ship sailed into New York harbor, and he was called upon deck to take his first view of the "land of the free"? At sight of the moving panorama of ships, tugs, and steamboats, I completely lost my self-possession, and actually did not know whether I was standing on my feet or on my head. I trembled and shook to such a degree that they thought I was going to faint, and led me to a seat. Whenever I cast my eyes on the Brooklyn Bridge, with its immense stones and wonderful mechanism, I thought God must have made it when he created the world. The hands of men could never have executed anything so immense and wonderful. The ship remained in the harbor for perhaps twenty-four hours, and during all that time nothing except a cup of coffee passed my lips. I was altogether too excited to eat. I did nothing but gaze around in wonder, and ask questions.

Everything was so new and strange, and all wonderful to me. The ship finally sailed into the dock. Here were in waiting several gentlemen. One of them, who had been sent from Lincoln University, took me and five of the other boys across to New Jersey on the ferry-boat, to where we were to board a train for Philadelphia. [In my first edition the number was printed twelve, when, as in this, it should have been five.] I was grown, but in all this time had never seen a railroad train, nor even conceived what it might be like.

We entered a car in the station and took our seats, I sitting in the same seat with Mr. Webb, the gentleman who had us in charge. I thought it to be a station-house or waiting-room of some kind, similar to the one in which we had waited for the ferry-boat on the New York side.

I asked Mr. Webb what we were going to travel in?

"In a train," he made answer. "What is a train?" I asked.

"You are in one now," he said with a smile. At that moment, it began slowly to pull out of the station. My limbs grew cold, and for an instant my heart ceased its beatings.

"Did I not tell you," he said, still smiling, "that this is a *train?* Do not feel alarmed; there is little if any danger. I have been over this road hundreds of times, and there has never yet been an accident." His words had no effect upon me. If he had escaped harm for so many times, then it was not to be expected that he should escape it for a longer period, and in all probability something terrible would happen to-night. I was terribly frightened. He tried to make me partake of some luncheon he had bought, but my tongue was parched with fear, and I motioned all food away from me in much disgust. As the train dashed along the track at a really terrific rate of speed, I expected every moment to have my brains knocked out. At length I reached forward and held the seat in front of me, as people tell me that drowning men catch at a straw; and I *never once loosened my hold.* Every time the train lurched in one direction, I would throw the weight of my body in the other direction, striving to the best of my ability to keep the car balanced.

Nothing that the gentleman could say or do could persuade me.

When we finally reached our destination I was completely exhausted and worn out, both in mind and in body, and I am sure that it is not to be wondered at.

We were taken to the private home of a gentleman in Philadelphia,—a beautiful home, the elegance and luxury of which filled us all with much surprise, and almost awe. How many times, in my clumsiness, I tripped over fancy-ribboned milking-stools, baskets, and hassocks.

My table manners, also, must have sorely offended the sensitive, refined tastes of our host and hostess and his one beautiful daughter, though I tried to put into practice all the points of etiquette given to me by the missionaries while at the mission. In the evening the gentleman's daughter played on the piano for us, and really, my old, wild, barbarous ideas took possession of my heart again as I saw the great "piece of wood" send out such delicious sounds simply because a young woman moved her hands to and fro. It was some time before I could be persuaded to approach a piano after that; not until I partly understood how the music was produced.

There was one thing, if no other, which we boys did enjoy and think a fine thing, and that was our soft beds. They were as easy, if not easier, than our native hammocks, was our conclusion, only I think you would have laughed could you have seen the manner in which some of them got into bed. We remained a day, at the end of which time we were taken to Lincoln University, and once again I had the same fear and difficulty with the cars.

We were assigned our rooms at the University. To say that I was homesick and lonely wouldn't be explaining the state of my feelings at all. We were the most miserable, wretched set of boys you ever saw. I was a curiosity to the other boys, who followed us about, laughed at my blunders,—which I dare say were many and comical enough,—and made remarks on our personal appearance in an off-hand way, and did not pause to consider our limited powers of understanding their tongue. I had thought that I was penned and shut up in the mission, but this life was so much more of a stived-up one that I wondered often how I could ever have thought that my freedom was cut off at the mission. I could not study. I would sit for hours over a book and never see a line in it; for my thoughts, oh! they were far away, miles away, far over the blue ocean, in the groves of the lovely land I had left. The hot tears would trickle over my cheeks at the thought.

There was no one here—no one who cared for me, whether I lived or whether I died; whether I learned my lessons or whether I did not; and the thought made me very sad. I missed Mrs. Roberts, who had been more than a mother to me, and Taradobah, who did really care for me almost as much as if I had been her own child. If there was only a friend such as they had been to me here in this land, I felt I could study harder, and apply myself more diligently. As it was, I could not, and did not; neither did any of the others. Our one desire was to get together and talk over home and the friends we had left behind. All these boys could not understand my dialect, and we had to speak English to one another.

Right here and now I want to correct a wrong conception of the copyist's, and one that has given me very much pain. It was a mistake in regard to the grand and good Lincoln University. My heart is with this old Institution, which I regard as the University of the American continent to solve the problem between the races. It is a University that has at its head a man of magnanimous heart, and a grand and loyal Christian. Indeed, I may say as much of the whole Faculty. They are all men whose highest aim is the elevation and uplifting of humanity, irrespective of physiognomy.

During my stay there Dr. Randall did everything to make it pleasant for me. I did not lack from him any attention that my physical, mental, or moral man required for advancement. I hope if any of the Faculty got hold of my first edition, that they will accept my apology in this. The lady who cut the book down was confused and made false statements about the University. Now to resume, I was sent to Wesleyan Academy. They put me on the cars in New York, and I came alone from there to Wilbraham, being placed under the care of the conductor. The cars did not terrify me so much as formerly; but I must have worried the conductor not a little, for I was anxious to get out at every station, thinking that I had reached my destination. "Wait, wait," he kept saying. "I will look after you; I will see that you are not carried past Wilbraham." But his words had no effect upon me. I kept bobbing up and down out of my seat every time the train slowed up.

After many hours' hard travel I finally did reach Wilbraham. The coachman helped me into a stage-coach that was in waiting, and told the driver to take me to Wilbraham Academy. It was quite dark, so that I was unable to see much of the surrounding country, and contented myself in the gloom of the coach as best I could. With a loud crack of his whip the driver drew up before a large building, shining with lamps. "Wesleyan Academy," he said, and helped me to alight. On the sidewalk in front of the building were many young ladies and gentlemen, strolling up and down, who stared at me curiously. I was shown into the pretty reception-room, and very soon a fine-looking old gentleman with a venerable gray beard came in and introduced himself. It was Doctor Steele, the principal of the Academy; and I felt my heart go out to him before he had spoken a half-dozen words. I felt that I had found a friend in this man, and I was not mistaken. I *had* indeed found a friend.

CHAPTER XV.

"Anything is possible for a man who knows his end,
And moves straight for it."

—Anon.

MY STRUGGLES FOR AN EDUCATION.

WILBRAHAM is a beautiful little town, skirted on the east by undulating hills and tree-crowned mountains, and on the west by long, lovely meadow lands. I could go out on the street and breathe a long, deep breath of pure, sweet air, and walk the hills and mountains, almost thinking at times that I was in my own beloved land.

I began to study immediately. The first term I took English grammar, composition, Latin grammar, and arithmetic. In my former edition there was a misstatement here in reference to the studies I pursued during my first term in this place. For one year the N. Y. S. C. S. encouraged me with words of commendation and good cheer, and paid all my expenses.

Wilbraham is a farming village, and I tramped from one end of it to the other, that summer, looking for work on some of the farms. At length one of the men hired me. I knew nothing about such work, for I had never been trained to do it; but I watched the others working beside me, and imitated them to the best of my ability. All through the hot month of July I worked out in the fields all day long; at the end of July my employer did not need my assistance further. I got jobbing work in the town for a little while. It was hard for me, because I was unused to anything like it. They were making alterations on Rich Hall, one of the Academy buildings, and I was put to work at pulling up the elevator. This I was obliged to do by sheer muscular strength, and it was no easy thing for one man to pull an elevator up a distance of about sixty or more feet, loaded, too, as it often was with a weight of a hundred and fifty pounds, more or less. My hands began to blister, but I persevered, and gritting my teeth stood the pain with some fortitude. At the end of two months, with much self-sacrifice and economy, I had managed to save fifty dollars. I could have worked no more at that time, for my hands had become so blistered and sore that I could hold nothing in them.

At the end of that time the board decided not to have any more young African men brought to this country, because after remaining for awhile here they were not willing to return to their own land to teach; and they also concluded to return to Africa all whom they had brought over within the year past, and have them educated at the college in Monrovia. I was one of those who were to be sent back. The treasurer of the board wrote to me to this effect, and that he would pay my expenses back to Africa. But I had made great sacrifices to come to America for an education. I had given up the prospect of being king of my tribe, and a business position where I was earning money while attending school at Monrovia; I had also paid my fare myself to America, using all the money I had saved in order to do this. I was also anxious to get a more thorough education than I could in the college at Monrovia, and especially to study in some theological school, which I could not do in Liberia, as there was none there. So I wrote to the treasurer that I *would not* return to my native shores until I had accomplished the ends for which I had sacrificed all my nearest interests, and come to a strange land among a strange people.

Then I went to New York to see H. M. ———, of the Colonization Society, and offered to give him a written agreement binding me to return to Africa after having finished my education, but he would not consent. At the same time I called upon the treasurer.

"Do you intend, Besolow," he asked me, "to remain in this country for good and all?"

"No, sir," I made reply; "I do not; but I do intend remaining here until I am properly prepared for the life-work which I have mapped out for myself in my native land among my people."

I left the gentlemen and went out upon the street.

Alone! I was indeed alone in that metropolis of America; and then I walked through that great city looking for something to do, whereby I might earn money to get something to eat. I went to the doors of several residences, asking of the persons who answered my pull at the bell for some work, anything by which I could earn some bread. But I was turned away, and told that they did not hire any colored help. Thus I went from house to house and from street to street, finding, in some cases, need of help; but because I was colored and had no friends I was branded, and there was no place for me. Oh, I thought, shall I die of hunger and neglect!

For a day and a half I traveled those streets; my feet were sore, and hurt me at every step. I could not buy any food for I had only enough money to get back to Wilbraham, where I knew if I utterly failed to get work the people would not let me starve.

At last a colored man took me to a colored Presbyterian church, and the minister gave me something to eat, and told me if I did not get work to return to him. He and his wife were very kind to me, but I was ashamed to live on their charity, and often went without my meals until I was so faint it seemed I must starve; then I would go back. By his questioning me we found that he and Hon. B. K. Anderson, who had helped me in arithmetic in Monrovia, were classmates.

After a time, by the aid of some other colored men, I got a job in a hotel to wait on the table. I did not know how,—I had never done anything of the kind,—but I must learn, so I went at it. After I had been working a few days I met with quite a mishap. A gentleman gave me an order, and I got it filled and brought it in on a waiter; but somehow I tipped the waiter and spilled the man's dinner over him. He was angry, and, with an oath, said to me, "What are you here for; you ought to be down South, on a plantation."

My pay was four dollars per week and one meal a day. I was told that I could eat all I wanted at that one meal, but could have no more. My room was four miles from my work, and I must walk twice a day when I could not pay for riding. This room was anything but comfortable, being infested with fleas and bed-bugs; the bed-clothing was not changed while I was there. Some nights I would get up on the foot-board to get away from my most uncomfortable bed-fellows.

One night one of the men with whom I worked wanted to to take me out and introduce me to his friends. I went, and was robbed of my ring, that I had brought from Monrovia, and the small amount of money I had been saving to carry me back to Wilbraham.

Well, time passed on. I worked here two months and had been able, after paying for my room, washing, and my scanty fare, to save five dollars. But I suffered loneliness, hunger, and disappointment. I wanted friends ; I wanted to get on, but I was failing ; and I was, oh, so heartsick.

Then out of the five dollars I possessed I paid my way back again to Springfield, though what I should do here I did not know. Nevertheless, with every passing moment my courage came back, and I thought of something one of the students had said to me in the year past: " Persevere, Besolow ; where there's a will there's always a way." With God's help and willingness, I would yet educate myself thoroughly. Doctor Steele, the only one to whom I could apply in my time of need, was away, traveling in the West. There was no one else. Friends, pray to God that you may never, never know the lonely hours that I knew for months ! "Alone !" Ah ! what sadder word is there in your language than that one, "alone"? Alone I was, save for the blessed presence of Christ my Saviour, who in that time of care and unhappiness was ever with me, saving me from committing many an act for which I would have been sorry afterwards.

I went to the Academy during the fall term of the next year, and I was dismissed by the N. Y. S. C. S., but winter came and my funds had given out again. Doctor Steele had returned from his Western trip, and in my trouble I went to him. In his great kindness of heart he permitted me to register for another term without pay in advance.

Things seemed to grow more hopeless and more gloomy every day, and only for the sweet love and strength of the Christ I leaned upon, I do not believe that I could have lived.

I have known days in the winter of '88 when I actually did not have one cent with which to buy a postal card to reply to the inquiring letters of my friends on the Liberian mission. My bare feet have been exposed to the cold and snow because of the holes in boots and stockings,—from this fact I have the rheumatism to-day,—and I have sat in the dark in my room for the want of a few cents to purchase oil. How often in the gloom of my room I have knelt to God and prayed for death. Those were in my discouraged moments. At other times I felt hopeful and cheerful, and had a faith in that proverb of yours, " The darkest hour is just before dawn."

The students, I dare to say, would have been glad to help me in my time of need, but I was proud, and they did not know of it; no one knew of all I suffered save myself and my Maker.

The pastor of the Methodist church in the village was the Rev. John R. Cushing, who is now pastor of a church on Stanton Avenue, Dorchester, Boston. Of this holy man I speak in all love and reverence; God bless him! If ever there was an earnest, devoted helper and counselor, if there was ever a man with heart like Christ, it is the reverend gentleman of whom I speak. Again I say, may God bless him, and shower upon him the choicest blessing of earth and of heaven!

"Besolow," he said to me one day, "why do you not prepare a lecture on Africa. It would be interesting to the people, I think."

At first I only smiled at his advice; but he was in earnest.

"You can do it," he said, "if you only think that you can."

I followed his advice, and did prepare one. Then, with his help and that of the Rev. Dr. Crowell, of Lynn, many places were secured for me, at which I lectured, with good enough success to encourage me.

Dr. Crowell was certainly a man of God. Many times when I was penniless, my clothes threadbare, my feet on the snow, he has helped me. He went from one charge to another, especially in the Springfield District, and he would never forget me, but would speak to benevolent men and women in my behalf. Through him many a time I have received shoes, clothing, and money.

When I heard of his illness my heart was filled with grief, and I feared exceedingly lest he should die. He did die, the dear old man; very suddenly and unexpectedly he entered that silent land from which "no traveler returns." His name shall ever be held dear and sacred to my memory. Had it not been for Doctor Crowell I never would have acquired that degree of self-confidence and self-reliance which I to-day possess. When I wrote to him and told him that the Colonization had dropped me, and that I was helpless in a strange land, he wrote me from Lynn, Mass., as nearly as I can remember, as follows:—

MY DEAR BESOLOW,—Remember that life is a journey, and a difficult one, which you must take bravely. Yes, life for many is a hard school. Sometimes everything appears easy, and delightful, and pleasing. All humanity and nature seems for us; and then, very suddenly, darkness, desolation, and discouragement stare us in

the face.   It is the gloom and hardships that make men and women
of us, not the fair prosperity.

You ask my advice about your remaining in America.   If I
were you I would remain.   It will be hard, I know; gloomy circumstances may attend you.   Stay and fight it through.   There is light
ahead.   Your brother in Christ,

L. CROWELL.

At the time of the help offered by Rev. J. R. Cushing and
Doctor Crowell, I was completely overwhelmed by debt; my
school bills had been mounting into a formidable sum, that took
my breath away when I thought about it ; and you may be sure
that I thought of it often enough.   That spring I lectured in
the vicinity of Boston and Springfield, and made enough
money to pay my expenses and go on with my studies.   I am
grateful to the Congregational, and Methodist, and Presbyterian
churches for the great help and kindness they have shown to
me ever since.   Those men who cast me off, will yet, please
God, see me returned to my native land with an education that
is worth something, and with a determination to use it for the
best good of my people.   They who supposed that I, enchanted
and captivated by American modes and manners of living,
would remain here always, will find out how mistaken they have
been.   I love America, and I will always love it ; but—I love
Africa more.

Sometimes when I look back and think of the trials I have
endured, I can plainly see the hand of God in it all, chasten-
ing, strengthening, and disciplining me ; and now I can truly
say that I am grateful to him, for sadly, indeed, did I need
these attributes.   Only trouble could have brought them.   I
was taught self-reliance in a way that, if hard, was still necessary.

I have lectured over the country from East to West, thus
having access to the people and to the various styles and methods of living ; my mind has been broadened as only travel—be
it ever so limited—can broaden the human mind and heart.   I
have been able to acquire a good deal of practical knowledge
of the Government, and have grasped, I think, the complete
and full sense of the word "civilization."   Ah ! I burn to see
the day when Africa, my Africa, will be revolutionized, and from
the Barbarys to the Cape, from ocean to ocean, know the meaning of that magic word as I know it.   After paying my expenses I save all that I can, till I am enabled to pay the passage

over to this country of a young brother and a nephew of mine, aged respectively twelve and thirteen years of age. Since my first edition, I am glad and grateful to say that I have had responses from various churches and benevolent men who have offered to pay the passage over to this country of those boys.

My own ambition, my own aim and desire, is to see Africa become a Christian nation. This is my chief thought by day and my dream by night. With this end in view I work, and pray, long and wait. "My land, my people!" is my watchword. God bless Africa!

Let the American churches speak out! Let the Congregationalists give a hearing! Hark! you, whose pilgrim fathers colonized New England shores, and there established freedom's glorious light! Let the solid army of the Congregationalists stand for the defense of the common faith, and tell heathen Africa that Calvary's work is finished! Let the cohort and the phalanx of Methodism come over to the "darkest Africa" and help its people out of the degradation of a polluted society, human sacrifices, and the burying alive of women in honor of heroes who have gone to Igenie. I call on Methodists because their lives are ever augmenting for the fight. Let the sons of the French Huguenot, the Presbyterians, give their brotherly hand,—they whose camp-fires glow in every nation under the canopy of God's heaven. Help the helpless and pity the dying.

Let the Baptists, whose ranks are still swelling with converts, help to the best of their ability in strengthening the faith of David, and stand firmly, truly, and valiantly for the defense of Israel.

Let the Episcopalian, whose camp-fire and altars glow brightly in the early dawn, and are preparing for that mighty day, save Africa's sons and daughters from the blood covenant and human sacrifices. Lutherans, we call upon you to dry our tears, and heal our wounds. You, whose name recalls the Reformation of dark ages, and made popes hear you, free Africa from *her* dark ways.

Let Congregationalists, Methodists, Presbyterians, and Baptists join hands fervently in this great work.

Let this very State, Massachusetts,—the seat of American liberty,—send floods of applications to Congress for the redemption of these most benighted men.

The grandest object that is before me is to enrich my mind and improve it; to unfold and invigorate the faculties; to store up in my mind the best and the most useful knowledge. I desire the most to nip and eradicate every bud of prejudice from my mind; to stay the tide of passion; to emancipate myself and soul from the race problem.

My intense desire is to elevate, and not pull down and destroy; to liberalize my view; subject my best power and every thought to empire of reason. I long to subordinate my best qualities for God's service; and, in short, to prepare for that silent and receding world. If I should wrong my fellow-man, an angry God I must face; so it behooves me to prepare the mortal for immortality, because, my fellow-man, " we shall meet a just God in that day."

My dear lovers of truth, this is my highest ideal of man and of life.

If any man loves to assail pride, egotism, prejudice, dogmatism, I do; on the other hand, if any love docility, meekness, kindness, affability, and liberality, I do.

BENDOO'S APPEAL.

O Spirit Divine! O Spirit anointing!
We on thee wait, and on us descend.
Myriads of Afric's sons are dying in darkness and sin,—
Jesus is calling;
    Whom shall Jesus send?
Ethiopia is beseeching with scarred hands and Arab's bondage.
    Whom shall Jesus send?
Rend, rend, O Christian, rend that long-enthralled chain.
Jesus is still gently calling;
    Whom shall Jesus send?

O Spirit Divine! O Spirit anointing!
Hear, oh hear the groan of Afric's swarthy sons,
With scarred hands and Arab's bondage!
Rend, O Christian! rend that long-enthralled chain.
Jesus is still tenderly calling;
    Whom shall Jesus send?
Look and see Africa unsealing gates;
Her nights of gloom are receding fast, and her sorrow is over.
Jesus is tenderly, gently pleading;
    Whom shall Jesus send?
Christian man, maiden, what a work that will be!
Dark Congo is breaking her chain of sin and errors,
And myriads of petitions to Jesus are now ascending,
Who, once on Calvary's cross bleeding, is now interceding.
    Whom shall Jesus send?
O young man, maiden, hear, oh hear!
The Spirit Divine calls you
To distant strand, to carry the gospel light, far, far away
Over the ocean deep.
Jesus is still quietly calling;
    Whom shall Jesus send?

Africa, my dearest! the land of heroic Stanley's pride,
Where the sky is brightest at eve, thy gloom of darkness is over:
A land fell in darkness, and blinded by error's chain,
Haste, O Christian, haste your aid to lend.
    Whom shall Jesus send?
The land of pyramids, ancient seat of science,
Fell into darkness by error's chain: dearest Africa, thy sorrow is over.
    Whom shall Jesus send?
A land once hating his cross, but now humbly waiting,
Gently bending at Jesus' calls,—

Haste, O Christian, haste your aid to lend;
Jesus is still eternally pleading.
    Whom shall Jesus send?
Africa, dearest! thy night of gloom and sorrow is over,
And thy sons shall be saved.
Haste, O Christian, haste the gospel to Afric's realms!
Carry them help, carry them healing,
"Far, far over the ocean deep;" Christian, pity them, pity them.
    Whom shall Jesus send?
Puritan sons, hear the appeal from this distant clime;
    Whom shall Jesus send?

Congregationalists, there is a pleasant land "far, far away,"
Where flowers eternally bloom by " breezes free," where " eternal
    harvest reigns,"
Where golden sand her coast doth surround,
And delicious fruits abound
Through long, hot summer days from " morn to noon, from noon to
    dewy eve;"
Where eternal spring abides, and " never-fading flowers";
Where the sun his equal ethereal course performs;
But the " Prince of Darkness" over this land doth reign.
    Whom shall Jesus send?
They lift their hands and raise their cry to Puritan sons.

O Christian, pity them; they are dying a thousand in a single day!
They are your brothers, sisters, and friends,
Will you let them to endless darkness go?
    Whom shall Jesus send?
My Christian brother, friend,
My countrymen are dying, oppressed in error's chain;
Pity, pity them, O Christian, pity them!
    Whom shall Jesus send?
Send the gospel light to Afric's realms,
Send them peace and love,—
The gracious proclamation that Calvary's works are finished.
Hear this appeal from Afric's pen, ye men and women!

[Postal address, Manoh, Salijah.]
SIERRA LEONE, WEST AFRICA,
Nov. 15, 1890.

DEAR MR. SHERMAN:—*

When I received your letter September 24th, last Saturday, I sent for your brother William, and asked whether he would like to go to America. He replied, If he had the money. So I told him to write to you. I hope he may give it in time for me to enclose in this.

You must indeed have been most industrious to have earned so much money; and it is a truly noble idea to educate your brother, who is a very good boy.

If you will get Messrs. Yates and Porterfield to give an order to their captain to take him over, I will see that he goes; but the vessels do not now call at Cape Mount, and if he has to go to Monrovia it will be very awkward; and should he have to walk the beach, he certainly ought to have ten days' notice.

Then he will want much warm clothing, which cannot be obtained here, even if we had the money; but having passed through the same experience, you will know what is needed.

I sent your letter to Mr. Coles, but have not seen him; he is seldom at home. I am sorry you troubled to send the dollar, but will keep it for William.

Wishing you every success, and God's choicest blessing of his Spirit, I am,   Yours sincerely,
M. R. BRIERLEY.

NOVEMBER 19, 1890.

PRINCE BESOLOW, Wesleyan Academy, Wilbraham, Mass.:

Dear Sir,—Since writing the accompanying, I find your brother William has drawn back, and it seems nothing can persuade him to change his mind; he says he cannot leave his mother. So, my poor friend, you must be content, and come out as soon as you can. We do not need high education, but God-fearing, pure-minded, conscientious men. This is, indeed, a grand field of labour, and labourers are needed. I shall hope to hear from you again; and tell me whether I shall give the dollar to your brother, or return it to you. Believe me,

Yours in sympathy,
M. R. BRIERLEY.

DEPARTMENT OF STATE,
     L. S.,
REPUBLIC OF LIBERIA.

MONROVIA, LIBERIA,
Feb. 18, 1891.

SIR: I am in receipt of your interesting letter of the 3d ulto., making inquiries with respect to the credibility of one Thomas Sherman, of the Vey tribe, and in reply will briefly say that I have known him for some years, and have heard of nothing to his discredit. He has been active, industrious, and honest, and, so far as

*English name given me on the Mission.

I have been able to discover, has always displayed a desire for the acquirement of useful knowledge.

I may further add that I knew Thomas Sherman's father, Chieftain Coirly, town of Bendoo, Fisherman's Lake, personally. I therefore recommend him to American confidence and benevolence, and you have my assurance that his tale is worthy of full faith and credit. I have not been favored with a copy of his book.

I remain, Sir,   Yours faithfully,
E. J. BARCLAY.
Secretary of State.

I hereby certify that the above is a true transcript of a letter received this day, March 28, 1891, the original of which remains in my possession.   WALTER LAIDLAW,

Pastor Jemain Memorial Church, West, Troy, N. Y.

SEAL.	Sworn to before me, this 30th day of March, 1891. F. B. DURANT, *Notary Public, Albany County.*

BAPTIST VEY MISSION,
MANOH SALIJAH, SIERRA LEONE, W. C. AFRICA,
February 18, 1891.

PRINCE BESOLOW:

Dear Friend,—Yours of Dec. 27, 1890, has been received, and contents noted with pleasure. We were truly glad to hear from you. We are pleased to see though you are in America, yet you remember Africa. We are all doing well in our mission work. The people of Bendoo have come together and built for me a church in the town at their expense, and I preach for them every Sunday. We have had a great many deaths in Bendoo the last year. Nearly every week some dies. Your uncle Wm. F. Cole is well, and sends how do to you.

It seems that the boys are not willing to go to America, nor are their people willing to give them up. Mr. Cole is willing, but he is alone. The old people say if you are so blessed of God, why don't you send them something. Well, Thomas, you know these people here. They want you to "dash" them; that is, they want you to send them something to beg them, as they call it. True, it is a bad thing to do to pay a man to let you do him good, but if you never send a " dash " to these old people, they will never let these boys go from here; you may talk till judgment day. Again, you must write them long, interesting letters. Tell them about the country and people. Tell them how you live, and how the people like you. And send them a " dash," and then I think you can get the boys.

Send the boys something. If they come to America, they need civilize clothes to wear in going. One of the boys, William ——, is at the Cape Mount Mission, and George is at Bendoo. I see him often. Mrs. Coles and our little daughter join me in much love to you. Hope you a great success.

I am yours in Christ,
JOHN J. COLES.

TO THE AMERICAN PEOPLE.

REALIZING that the Christian public is pressed on all sides for benevolences, I came before you with plans for gospel mission work, only asking that you consider them, and if they meet your approval as being advisable and feasible, I ask your sympathy and such aid as God may give you ability to render. You can at least pray for the work.

When I left Liberia, God laid it upon my heart to get an education in America and carry back to that benighted land that which would elevate her people,—namely, a school.

I now purpose to establish a school in Guinea, Africa, for the evangelization of the black people of West Africa. The character of this school is to be both educational and missionary, whereby I hope to bring a Christian civilization to this people. It is my purpose to establish, in connection with the school, a church, and make the Gospel of Jesus Christ the great central theme in the work. There will be a farm connected therewith, which will help to make the school self-supporting.

After careful consideration and prayer the institution is named Bendoo University and Great Britian and the American School of Missions, for which I have 200 acres of land,—the gift of the son of King Armah of Guinea. We have privilege of selecting the location, which will be on the high lands, for the benefit of the workers,—the high land a cool climate, in which foreigners can live with little danger to health.

Donations already received amounted to $1,500.25 : from Liberia, $500.25, from Americans, $1,000.20. Pledges have been received from benevolent Americans for $4,002.16, and our friends in the British Empire will soon respond with their gift, as I am now holding correspondence with prominent men in England and Belgium in behalf of the University. So the year 1891 opens with the following to the credit of the institution :—

Land in Liberia, very productive, estimated value,		$500.00
Liberian Contributions	. . . . .	500.25
American Contributions	. . . . .	1,000.20
American Pledges	. . . . .	4,002.16
	Total,	$6,002.61

To this will be added the profit from the sale of this book. And in order that every man, woman, and child may have a chance to contribute to this work, cards will be published, bearing the picture of a brick of this institution, which will be sold for ten cents, the profits going into the school fund. One million cards represent the bricks of the institution.

For reference of character and reliability, I refer, by permission, to,—

REV. ADDISON P. FOSTER, D.D., Pastor of Immanuel Congregational Church, Roxbury, Mass., and REV. JOHN R. CUSHING, A.M., Pastor Methodist Episcopal Church, Mattapan, Mass., Treasurers of the funds for the mission school.

REV. G. M. STEELE, D.D., LL.D., President Wesleyan Academy, Wilbraham, Mass.

HON. A. D. WILLIAMS, Senator, Monrovia, Liberia, Africa.

E. J. BARCLAY, Secretary of State.

HON. ROBERT T. SHERMAN.

A few Christian young men uniting with me, have organized to carry forward this work; to raise the money, and build this Gospel Lighthouse for West Africa. · We ask whoever reads this to do three things for us: first give us your prayers that God may give us strength to do this great work, and that the people may become interested in the work; then buy this book, and ask others to buy it; do the same with the "Brick Cards," remembering that the profits go to the mission-school fund; and lastly, if God has blessed you with this world's goods, and if you want to help tell the story of salvation to the dark sons of Africa, give to this work as God has prospered you. And when from the east and from the west, from the north and from the south, we meet to sit down with patriarchs, and prophets. and the ransomed of all nations, you may know some one personally from the bounds of this now benighted land whom you helped to a saving knowledge of Jesus. May Christian women and men of all denominations pray for this light to Darkest Africa.

All Sunday-school superintendents are invited to help by sending for these cards and introducing them in their schools. Do something for the Dark Continent while you have so glorious an opportunity.

I do hereby most heartily and sincerely acknowledge my indebtedness to Rev. Benjamin F. Gill, A.M., my teacher in Greek and history. I feel myself under many obligations to him for the instruction I have received under him. I realize that I am better in every respect for having come in contact with the honorable gentleman. Although I am looking forward to other fields of labor, yet I will remember him and the time he spent on me. I shall ever be mindful of the man as a gentleman. May he live long and enjoy life. I say again and again, many thanks to him: when my enemies would sap my very vitality, he fought to save me. I remember when I had no money to buy my Greek books. and had made up my mind to give up the study, he offered to purchase them for me. May he think he has done something for my land. I shall always remember him with a grateful mind.

Let me not forget my friends in Boston and West Troy who protected me when, through my own carelessness and negligence, I fell into intricable difficulties, Messrs. Geo. A. White, I. N. F. Thayer, Frank Wood, and finally Rev. Mr. Walter Laidlaw. These gentlemen saved me. Many thanks to them; and may God bless my enemies, if I have any.

I take the opportunity, also, to thank my other teachers, namely, Charles H. Raymond, A.M., B. S. Annis, A.M., Joseph C. Rockwell, A.M., and especially John F. Mohler, A.M. Also extend my hearty appreciation to my friends of fidelity, Misses A. M. Hall, Emily L. Wyman, and particularly Sarah Loomis.

One word more for the book. The subjects are not arranged chronologically, and there are great intervals which are not filled out.

CORRECTIONS.

On pages vii and viii of the preface, and 32, 37, and 49 of the book, I have called attention to errors made in the old book; in addition to these I find there are still some statements that should have been corrected, but were overlooked. These are due to the same cause for their original appearance as those corrected in the text. See pages noted below.

Much of this trouble arose from my telling my assistant stories of both my grandfather and my brother, whose names were like my own,—Besolow; and she, mixing the incidents of my own life with these stories, has made some grave errors appear.

Pages 15 and 29: The punishments here spoken of are facts, but the stories are drawn rather stronger than perhaps they should have been.

Page 33: A story told me; I know nothing of the real facts.

Page 47: I was in the hunting school, but did not take the active part in some of the work as represented; all, however, was true of the school as a whole.

· Page 51: Boys were not allowed to engage in the elephant hunt; none but old hunters did this.

Page 56: "One foot was partly devoured," should read, one foot was partly destroyed.

Pages 66 and 67: " Swelled to almost double his natural size," is, of course, an exaggeration.

Page 78: " Fifteen hundred boys "—an estimated number.

Pages 83 and 84: These slaughtered men were not our own soldiers, but were mercenaries who were hired, and who turned traitor: in the battle.

Page 101: "Dozens of infants," should read, dozens of animals; and "prisoners innumerable," should be, sacrifices innumerable.

The "Amazon story," of Chapter VII. in the old book, was only a story told me by my father of my grandfather's days; but, without my consent, was so badly mixed up with my own history as to spoil whatever of truth there was in it. I have decided to leave it out of this edition. The reference to it on page 88 is accounted for by this note.

Page 110: The " proclamation " is given (in substance) as near as I can remember it.

THOS. EDWARD BESOLOW.